P9-CFR-021

CHERRY AMES, CHIEF NURSE

CHERRY AMES
CHIEF NURSE

By

HELEN WELLS

SPRINGER PUBLISHING COMPANY

New York

Copyright © 1944 by Grosset & Dunlap, Inc.
Copyright © renewed 2006 by Harriet Schulman Forman
Springer Publishing Company, Inc.

All rights reserved. No part of this publication may be
reproduced stored in a retrieval system, or transmitted
in any form or by any means, electronic, mechanical,
photocopying, recording, or otherwise, without the
prior permission of Springer Publishing Company, Inc.

Springer Publishing Company, Inc.
11 West 42nd Street, 15th Floor
New York, NY 10036-8002

Production Editor: Print Matters, Inc.
Cover design by Takeout Graphics, Inc.
Composition: Compset, Inc.

06 07 08 09 10/5 4 3 2

Library of Congress Cataloging-in-Publication Data

Wells, Helen, 1910–
   Cherry Ames, chief nurse / by Helen Wells.
      p. cm. — (Cherry Ames nurse stories)
   Summary: Now chief of her unit in the Army Nurse Corps, Cherry Ames
has the support of her Spencer Hospital friends as she strives to meet the
challenge of organizing an evacuation hospital on a Pacific island.
   ISBN 0-97715-973-6 (pbk.)
   [1. Nurses—Fiction. 2. Hospitals—Fiction. 3. World War,
1939-1945—Fiction. 4. United States. Army Nurse Corps—Fiction.
5. Islands of the Pacific—History—20th century—Fiction.] I. Title.

PZ7.W4644Cd 2005
[Fic]—dc22

2005051740

Printed in the United States of America by Bang Printing

Contents

Foreword

Helen Wells, the author of the Cherry Ames stories, said, "I've always thought of nursing, and perhaps you have, too, as just about the most exciting, important, and rewarding, profession there is. Can you think of any other skill that is *always* needed by everybody, everywhere?"

I was and still am a fan of Cherry Ames. Her courageous dedication to her patients; her exciting escapades; her thirst for knowledge; her intelligent application of her nursing skills; and the respect she achieved as a registered nurse (RN) all made it clear to me that I was going to follow in her footsteps and become a nurse—nothing else would do. Thousands of other young people were motivated by Cherry Ames to become RNs as well. Cherry Ames motivated young people on into the 1970s, when the series ended. Readers who remember reading these books in the past will enjoy rereading them now—whether or not they chose nursing as a career—and perhaps sharing them with others.

My career has been a rich and satisfying one, during which I have delivered babies, saved lives, and cared for people in hospitals and in their homes. I have worked at the bedside and served as an administrator. I have published journals, written articles, taught students, consulted, and given expert testimony. Never once did I regret my decision to enter nursing.

During the time that I was publishing a nursing journal, I became acquainted with Robert Wells, brother of Helen Wells. In the course of conversation I learned that Ms. Wells had passed on and left the Cherry Ames copyright to Mr. Wells. Because there is a shortage of nurses here in the US today, I thought, "Why not bring Cherry back to motivate a whole new generation of young people? Why not ask Mr. Wells for the copyright to Cherry Ames?" Mr. Wells agreed, and the republished series is dedicated both to Helen Wells, the original author, and to her brother Robert Wells who transferred the rights to me. I am proud to ensure the continuation of Cherry Ames into the twenty-first century.

The final dedication is to you, both new and old readers of Cherry Ames: It is my dream that you enjoy Cherry's nursing skills as well as her escapades. I hope that young readers will feel motivated to choose nursing as your life's work. Remember, as Helen Wells herself said: there's no other skill that's *"always* needed by everybody, everywhere."

Harriet Schulman Forman, RN, Ed.D.
Series Editor

CHAPTER I

Jungle Christmas

CHERRY AMES STOOD UNDER A PALM TREE SOMEWHERE in the Pacific, the day after Christmas. The officer who had just helped her off the plane said, "Stay here in the shade. Now if you will please excuse me for a minute—" and walked away. Cherry watched him go and squinted through the heat haze at the parked Army bomber which had brought her here this afternoon. "Of all places for me to be spending Christmas!" she thought. "I've crossed the international date line and lost a day, so I'll count today Christmas. But of all the un-Christmas-y places! I've read about romantic tropic isles, but I never thought I'd get to one *this* way!"

She pulled down the trim jacket of her nurse's olive drab uniform, and set the jaunty cap more firmly on her black curls. Cherry's eyes were black too, large and

1

sparkling, thoughtful but full of fun—brilliant red cheeks and lips and a warmhearted smile lived up to the lively promise of those eyes. She knew perfectly well, of course, that a nurse, and especially an Army nurse, can, in the course of duty, nonchalantly pop up in any corner of the world. "But I wish," she thought, "that someone would kindly tell me what I'm here *for!*"

She had been an Army nurse only four months. Her first foreign assignment had been with her own Spencer Hospital unit at the Army hospital in Panama. Suddenly she had been ordered to pack her things and to be ready to board a plane which was leaving in an hour. Then for twenty-four hours she was whisked through empty skies over the Pacific. Now she had been set down on this island—all without a word of explanation. Cherry felt distinctly breathless. She did know that she was to deliver a new serum to research doctors here who were seeking new ways to fight malaria. But that would take only a few minutes. After that, on what new adventure would the Army Nurse Corps send her?

Cherry stared at the first hibiscus blossom she had ever seen, then glanced up into the tree hoping to see a monkey or at least a coconut. She looked around inquisitively. To one side were hospital and Army buildings, beyond lay the Pacific, ahead rose the jungle. She certainly was a long way from Hilton, Illinois, her home town.

Cherry was on Port Janeway, one of the larger islands which dot the vast Pacific Ocean. These islands, like a chain of irregularly-spaced steppingstones, lead to war-making Japan. There were few signs of Christmas, much less a white Christmas, on this hot jungle island, with its fortifications, its wooden base hospital buildings, thatched huts, and sound of distant gunfire. Port Janeway, recaptured from the enemy, was being used as a resting place for the hard-pressed or wounded American soldiers who were driving the enemy off the forward islands.

A young officer burst out of the door of the largest hut. "Lieutenant Ames!" he called.

"Yes, sir!" Cherry responded quickly.

"You will please come with me," the aide directed.

Cherry gulped and followed him. The aide was leading her into Medical Headquarters. Here came her fate!

Cherry entered the office and stood at attention. Before the desk stood a thin, long-bodied, short-legged man. He had small dark eyes, and a lone thatch of yellow hair stood up on his head. He reminded Cherry irresistibly of a stork. Beside him stood another officer, a doctor, for he wore the gold caduceus of the Army Medical Corps.

The aide presented Cherry. "Colonel Pillsbee, this is Lieutenant Ames, awaiting orders. Lieutenant Ames, your new Commanding Officer."

Lieutenant-Colonel Pillsbee cocked his head, saluted, and Cherry saluted in return. Then he held out his hand. "How do you do, Lieutenant Ames. I am glad you arrived safely," he said stiffly. "Major Pierce, Lieutenant Ames."

The Major was a handsome, graying, easy-mannered man. Cherry liked the way his eyes and mouth crinkled up in a genial smile, and the substantial, comfortable look of him. He shook hands with Cherry as if trying to put her at her ease. "You're going to hear some news, Lieutenant!"

Cherry's black eyes widened. Colonel Pillsbee cleared his throat, then announced in a cultivated, precise voice:

"Lieutenant Ames, Major Pierce has informed me that he has received orders from Washington that you are to be promoted to the rank of acting Chief Nurse, and first lieutenant."

"Oh!" She was going to be Chief Nurse! Her mind was racing. So this is what Colonel Wylie had hinted at when he said, back in Panama, "An important promotion and a new post await you." Cherry had expected a promotion to first lieutenant, but she had never dreamed of this added distinction. Chief Nurse! Chief of what? Where? Wasn't she going to work with Spencer unit and her old nurse friends any more?

Major Pierce grinned. "Congratulations, Lieutenant Ames." Cherry trembled while Major Pierce pinned a silver bar on her shoulder.

"Th—thank you, sir," Cherry said shakily. They shook hands all around, stiff Colonel Pillsbee, easy-going Major Pierce, and a very red-cheeked Cherry.

"The rank of *acting* Chief Nurse," Colonel Pillsbee observed, "is—er—similar to a probationary status."

Cherry sobered. "I understand, sir," feeling some advance worry at the new responsibilities which, she knew, accompanied her proud new bar.

"Spencer unit is being brought here from Panama," Colonel Pillsbee explained solemnly. When she heard this, Cherry's spirits soared. Then she would continue to work with Ann and Gwen and all the rest of her old classmates! The Commanding Officer continued, "Ordinarily the unit would stay in Panama a year, but there is an even more serious nurse shortage here. Colonel Wylie will not head the unit as formerly. Major Pierce will be the new Spencer unit director."

Cherry involuntarily turned to smile at jolly Major Pierce, and received a twinkle in reply. She was glad he was to be her superior officer, though she suspected she would miss the quick-tempered Colonel Wylie with whom she had clashed so often in the past.

"But what about Major Joseph Fortune?" Cherry asked anxiously for her old friend. "And Captain Lex Upham? Won't they continue to be part of the Spencer unit?"

"No," said Colonel Pillsbee, "Major Pierce is getting fifty new men, doctors, and some technicians. There will be the original sixty nurses from Spencer Hospital and Nursing School. The nurses are in your charge now, Lieutenant Ames. Also there will be about two hundred corpsmen to assist the nurses. We estimate that—Major Pierce, have you the figures here?"

While the two officers studied some papers, Cherry thought of Dr. Joe, who had inspired her to enter nursing, and of her particularly good friend, Lex. Brilliant, headstrong, unpredictable, lovable Lex! She remembered how, when she was a student nurse, and she and Lex were just getting to know each other, she had helped clear Lex of the ugly suspicions surrounding him when Dr. Joe's formula was stolen and circumstantial evidence pointed to Lex's possible guilt. But it was Lex who had come to her aid in Panama, who had loyally helped her to solve the mystery of the Indian. Cherry thought of the ring he had offered her—twice—and smiled ruefully. She wanted to accept Lex's ring some day. But now she had been sent here to the Pacific, and Dr. Joe and Lex were not coming! Cherry was sharply disappointed. She supposed Dr. Joe and Lex were assigned to do research. But she had no chance to ask the Commanding Officer about this, for he had turned to her again, papers in hand.

"—thus our evacuation unit," Colonel Pillsbee summed up in his hesitant, chilly voice, "can take care of seven hundred to a thousand patients." Cherry's mind reeled as she heard those figures.

The Commanding Officer looked at Cherry critically. "Do you think you can successfully supervise so many patients and nurses, Lieutenant Ames?"

Cherry swallowed. It was exactly what she herself was wondering. "I'll try my very best, sir," she promised earnestly.

There was a doubtful pause, while Colonel Pillsbee studied Cherry's young and pretty face. She wished desperately that Major Pierce would say something comforting and reassuring, such as "Her superiors would not recommend a promotion if her record did not merit it" or "Her youth is not necessarily against her." But the surgeon did not interrupt his superior officer.

"Our evacuation unit," Colonel Pillsbee continued, "will proceed within a few weeks to Pacific Island 14, on the edge of combat area. There are infantry, anti-aircraft, and other installations on the island. I am Commanding Officer of Pacific Island 14, and also of adjoining Islands 13 and 15."

Cherry tried to look intelligent. She did not under stand clearly what all this meant, except that they were going to be up near the fighting, and that this stern and hard-bitten old warrior was in charge of everyone and everything.

"Well, young lady," Major Pierce asked cheerfully, "do you think you're going to like running an evacuation hospital?"

Cherry melted at his warm and human tone of voice. "I've never seen an evacuation hospital, sir."

The Commanding Officer frowned slightly at that.

Major Pierce smiled his easy smile. "Very simple. It's a big, rough, but complete hospital, quite near the fighting, so that we can evacuate—bring out— the wounded from battle *promptly.* It's supposed to be more or less mobile, and we *can* pack up and move in a day, but it's too big a hospital to move around much. So we'll pick a good jungle spot and stay put as long as there is fighting in that general area."

"A complete hospital will suddenly grow out of the wilderness!" Cherry breathed. She thought of the soldiers fighting out there who would know that the Medical Corps was standing by, ready to take care of them. Suddenly she was grateful that she was a nurse—not only for the adventure which loomed ahead, but for the lives she could save and the courage she could bring. Her dark eyes shone.

Colonel Pillsbee glanced at her even more dubiously, and now he was looking over papers which Cherry knew must be her records. Another awful silence fell. Finally Colonel Pillsbee folded his hands on his knobby knees, and enunciated carefully:

"Frankly, Lieutenant Ames, you are too young to have had much nursing experience. Moreover, your extreme youth and your—er—attractive appearance suggest that you may not be quite the right person for this most serious work. I ought to warn you that you will not find it—er—glamorous."

Cherry suppressed a flare-up of anger. And then, suddenly, she felt hurt and belittled. "I assure you, sir," the words rushed out, "I am not looking for glamour. I am perfectly responsible and serious. Perhaps my appearance is misleading, sir." Major Pierce chuckled. "But I'm sure that I can prove myself, Colonel Pillsbee. I will work very hard to deserve the rank of Chief—acting Chief Nurse." Though she did not show it, Cherry was close to tears.

The Commanding Officer said dryly, "Very well, Lieutenant Ames. That will be all for this afternoon. Major Pierce will discuss further unit matters with you later."

Out on the doorstep of the hut, Cherry took a deep breath. Too young and pretty, huh? So he had challenged her, had he? All right! She'd prove to Colonel Pillsbee—and to herself—that she could be a good Chief Nurse! She'd prove that she could run an evacuation unit! The sun glinted on her new silver bar. Chief Nurse! Cherry filled again with happiness at her wonderful new honor. She looked excitedly into the dark jungle, across the inscrutable sea.

"Lieutenant Ames?" Cherry found a friendly nurse smiling at her.

"Yes, I'm Lieutenant Ames," Cherry smiled back.

"I'm the assistant to the Chief Nurse here. I'll show you to your quarters. You must want to rest a little after that long flight."

The two young women walked past the wooden hospital buildings together. "I'd like to congratulate you, Lieutenant," the Janeway nurse said.

Cherry was grateful. And in Nurses' Quarters other nurses congratulated her, too. But how she wished her family were here, instead of only strangers, to rejoice with her!

At supper in the big mess hall that evening, Cherry found herself surrounded by doctors and nurses and soldiers, pressing their congratulations upon her. They weren't strangers, really! "We Medical Corps people are one large family, all over the world," Cherry realized warmly. Between meeting the friendly hospital staff, and her excitement, the new Chief Nurse was not able to eat much supper. Her promotion was a grand Christmas present! This certainly was one Christmas she would never forget!

The first thing Cherry did next morning was to cable the wonderful news, and her new APO address, to her family. Then she went back to her tiny room in the Army Nurses' Quarters and wrote her parents the details in a V-mail letter. She wrote her flier brother Charlie a V-mail, too.

That done, Cherry took out her last letters from home and re-read them once again.

"#zWe ear all well? h0pe you are foo," her father had typed with one finger, in his real estate office. Cherry giggled; she was pretty sure her father had chuckled himself. He wrote—laboriously—that the whole family did volunteer work at Hilton Clinic, now considerably understaffed because so many doctors and nurses had gone to war.

She turned next to her mother's letter. She could almost see her pretty, youthful, brown-eyed mother sitting very erect at the mahogany desk in the blue-and-mahogany living room, writing very deliberately, pausing to glance out of the window at the peaceful, small-town street. It would be white and hushed now with snow, the big oaks in front of the Ames's house sheathed in ice. Holly wreaths would hang in the neighbors' windows and on front doors, before snowy porch steps. Cherry glanced out of her own window at a waving palm tree silhouetted against the hot purple sky, and sighed.

Her mother wrote that Cherry's own little room still had its crisp white curtains and white dressing-table skirt, with its red bows, and that Cherry's room was the one thing Midge took good care of.

Cherry grinned. Irrepressible Midge Fortune, five years younger than herself, was almost Cherry's kid sister. Cherry had kept an eye on her ever since Mrs. Fortune died. She had kept an eye on Dr. Fortune, too, so lost in his brilliant medical research that he neglected practical matters. Dr. Fortune—Dr. Joe, Cherry affectionately called him—meant a great deal to her. Friend and neighbor all her life, he had shown her the great idealistic service of medicine, and encouraged her to enter nursing. It was a real loss to Cherry that he, and his assistant, young Captain Lex Upham, were leaving the unit. She would miss them, Lex especially.

"Still," Cherry mused, "I suppose they're such valuable research scientists, they'll be more useful to the Army in a laboratory at home than in a hospital in the combat zone." In any case, Cherry figured, Dr. Joe would remain away from Hilton, and Midge would go on living with Cherry's parents. Midge kept things lively in the Ames household with her harum-scarum exploits—sometimes lively to the point of bedlam. Cherry hoped her mother would survive Midge.

Last, Cherry picked up Charlie's tiny, closely-written V-mail letter. Her twin brother, though he was as blonde as she was dark, wrote real news this time. An aerial gunner in the Army Air Forces, he had just transferred from combat flying to the Air Transport Command. "Don't tell Mother but this is just as dangerous as combat duty," he wrote. "We'll be ferrying—that is, delivering—men and supplies through enemy territory to our troops in China and Alaska and Africa, wherever they need things fast. Fast means planes. That's us— ATC. Wish me good luck. How are you, pal?"

Cherry smiled. She certainly missed her brother. It would be wonderful if one day his plane were to swoop down out of the blue Pacific sky and land on Island 14. Well, in the Army, anything was possible. She wondered where Charlie was. No telling. He could be anywhere on the globe a plane could take him, anywhere an S O S called him.

Cherry was proud she was an Army nurse. Once she would have worried her heart out about her brother, but fighting as a nurse was a great deal more to the point than staying home and worrying. Not that Cherry did not love Hilton—she was homesick this very minute, in this barracks room, on this exotic island. But it was to save her home, and all it stood for, that she was here.

"Shucks," she thought, "war or no war, I'd be a nurse anyway." Nursing—restoring health and giving peace of mind to the sick—was the most exciting thing in Cherry's life. For Cherry knew that, in peace just as much as in war, the world needs brave and understanding girls in that most feminine, most humane, and most beloved of all professions.

Cherry glanced at her nurse's watch on her wrist, and hastily put her letters away in her small suitcase. She had an appointment with Major Pierce!

That afternoon, and daily for the rest of the week, Cherry worked with Major Pierce to prepare for the unit's trek into the jungle. There was a quantity of new equipment to be checked, many plans to be laid, many records to be gone over. Cherry found this routine work dull, but she soon saw its results.

One morning a small group of officers and enlisted men set out into the jungle, alone, unarmed, with portable hospital equipment slung over their shoulders. "Advance detail," Major Pierce said, as he and Cherry stood watching them go. "Getting things ready for the rest of us." They headed for Island 14 and the sound of those distant guns.

She had seen another example of unselfish courage when she delivered Dr. Joe's new serum to his research colleagues working here. Six privates had volunteered to expose themselves to fever, for the sake of research and saving other lives.

Toward the end of that remarkable week, a ship docked. That afternoon, in the Red Cross canteen, Cherry waited to meet fifty new doctors who were joining her unit.

"It will take me some time to remember all their names!" she confessed to Major Pierce, seeing the crowd of doctors in khaki.

"Don't worry, you'll learn them gradually," the unit director said. Cherry grinned her thanks. "Anyhow, you won't have many dealings with the doctors. That's my department. You'll just deal directly with me on any doctors' matters. The nurses are your department."

So Cherry said fifty how-do-you-do's and hoped none of the new doctors thought her, as Colonel Pillsbee did, too young and pretty for her post. To her relief, all the officers seemed to accept her as Chief Nurse without any raised eyebrows.

At the end of the second hard-working week, another ship docked. This time Cherry was waiting at the pier. She felt very happy indeed as the gangplank was swung up to the ship, and her old classmates, in their nurses' olive drab, came running down. "We heard about you, Ames!" they cried, laughing. "Hurray for you, Cherry!" "Hey, girls, look at our new boss!"

All sixty of them crowded around her on the pier, ignoring the jeeps and trucks they were blocking. "It's marvelous," redheaded Gwen Jones declared, "but you'd better treat us right!"

"Well, if you think you're going to discipline *us!*" Ann Evans teased. "And where are we headed?"

By this time, exasperated jeep drivers were shouting at them. Cherry said hastily, "Step right this way, ladies, and your brand-new acting Chief Nurse will reveal all." She thought, as she shooed the girls into the waiting automobiles, "There's no use trying to sound formal with them—they'd tease me from here to Tokyo!"

After a brief drive, the girls surged into the canteen. They perched themselves around the room and cried mercilessly, "Speech! Speech!"

Cherry stood up at the front of the room, and for a moment she was frightened. They were old friends, good nurses and good soldiers, but would she be able to manage sixty high-spirited girls? Here and there she saw a few envious or resentful glances. Her first words, which the girls were waiting for, would count heavily. Cherry dug her hands into her pockets and began.

"We've been in some strange places together," she started, "but now we are going into the strangest and most dangerous place so far—into the jungle." Then she told them all she had learned those two hard-working weeks from Major Pierce. "It sounds exciting, but it's going to be the hardest thing we've ever done."

The girls' eyes sparkled, listening. Even quiet Mai Lee's little ivory face was excited. Only Josie Franklin, shrinking behind her glasses, looked doubtful. When Cherry said, "We'll take care of seven hundred to a thousand soldier patients," delighted rueful groans and "Whee! *Us!* Imagine!" came from all over the room.

"I guess that covers all the facts," Cherry finished. "And now there's something else I want to say." The girls waited expectantly. "It's about—well—the Chief Nurse might have been any of you just as well as me,"

Cherry said modestly. "And if it seems funny to you to have me for a Chief Nurse, it seems even funnier to *me*. After all, we've been partners in plenty of scrapes, and now I'm supposed to discipline you!" She grinned uncertainly, and the girls grinned back. "A Chief Nurse is supposed to be a stonyhearted slave driver. You needn't worry about that, but of course we *must* have discipline, for the sake of the work we're going to do. I am asking you," Cherry said gravely, "to give me your cooperation, not so much to me personally, as to the authority of the Chief Nurse's job." She looked appealingly into the familiar, listening faces.

"Gosh, I don't have to make any speeches to *you*. We've all always worked together beautifully. All we have to do is keep up our same good teamwork. We're nurses, we all know we have most urgent business ahead of us. We nurses are the only women who go right up front with the soldiers. If we weren't serious, we wouldn't have taken the Army oath, or the Florence Nightingale pledge, in the first place. I don't have to remind you," Cherry said with some difficulty, and her voice dropped, "that we are here to dedicate our lives so that others may live."

There was a deep silence in the room. The girls looked so shaken that Cherry tried for a lighter tone.

"Frankly, I've got a humdinger of a responsibility. You all have to help me by cooperating like *mad!*"

Voices came from all sides of the room. "Okay, we will!" "Don't worry, Cherry, we're with you!" "You can count on us!" And then, she realized, that wave of sound was—of all things—applause!

It was all right. It was wonderful. The girls were with her completely—even if Colonel Pillsbee was not.

~~~~~~

CHAPTER II

Leapfrog

AN AWFUL CATERWAULING BROKE THE DAWN STILLNESS. Out of the door of the Commanding Officer's hut, Colonel Pillsbee's head emerged. He blinked in the early greenish light and shouted above the howling harmonies:

"Who is making those unearthly noises?"

The song, such as it was, petered out. There stood the nurses, ready to go, dressed in their stout olive drab trousers and blouses, complete with leggings, high field shoes, helmets, and packs on backs.

"It's a serenade, sir," came a muffled voice from the rear. The girls' sleepy faces were perfectly innocent—except Cherry's. Fortunately, she thought, Colonel Pillsbee did not yet know Gwen Jones's voice. Unfortunately, he would blame any pranks of the nurses on the Chief Nurse.

"I don't care to be serenaded," Colonel Pillsbee snapped.

Another uncertain voice came from the ranks. "We were serenading Major Pierce, sir. Today is his birthday."

Colonel Pillsbee stared at them icily, then stated, "In future, have some respect for rank! There will be no more of these undignified demonstrations! Be ready to stand inspection! We start in an hour," and retreated into his hut.

And then, to their chagrin, an aide told them that Major Pierce had been at the other end of camp for the past hour.

Cherry scolded her nurses as they held out their mess gear for breakfast, on line at the cook tent.

"It's your own fault," Ann Evans said. Her dark blue eyes and smooth brown hair were as unruffled as herself. "You made us get up an hour too early."

Plump, comfortable Bertha Larsen declared, "Colonel Pillsbee was not very nice; he just hasn't a sense of humor."

"We-ell," said Gwen. She grinned, and even her short red hair and the sprinkling of freckles on her merry face seemed to laugh too. "If you had just let us sleep, boss——"

Cherry, who was so often late herself, had taken no chances on having her nurses late this all-important morning. For today the unit started out for Pacific Island 14. For four days, the newly arrived nurses had lived in a tented staging area, while they received special instruction for jungle duty. The diligent new Chief Nurse had seen to it that every girl had full equipment, and was properly warned to expect mosquitoes, mud, and no desserts.

They were going to march by a special plan, which Cherry called "leapfrog." Colonel Pillsbee thought that, as long as the unit would be passing through lonely outposts on its long march across Janeway Island, they should stop and treat the soldiers stationed en route. Because these soldiers en route were in small temporary groups, as work battalions, and were moved around so often, no field hospital was set up for them. But they did need care. On the other hand, since the evacuation unit was too huge to act as a field hospital for these small groups of soldiers, the whole unit would not be needed at any one outpost. Chief Nurse Ames had thereupon invented her system of "leapfrog." Cherry suggested that the medical unit start out together but split into three sections on the way. Each section would stop at only one outpost, then catch up with the others. Thus they could save time and still wind up the march together. It should take them three days, two days to march, one day to set up medical tents and work. Colonel Pillsbee gave Cherry the first approving look she had had from him, and adopted her "leapfrog" plan.

"Why couldn't we sail around the island," Vivian Warren wanted to know, "instead of hiking across it?"

Marie Swift sniffed. "Did you see those coral reefs around the island? You can't sail anywhere near the island. And how'd you like to sail in open sea, with Jap fighter planes taking pot shots at you?"

"Besides," Cherry added, "the men in Janeway jungle need our medical care."

So on this cloudy morning, a long column of doctors, corpsmen, and nurses, all in olive drab work suits and helmets, were leaving civilization to start their long trek through the jungle.

The evacuation unit still lacked another X-ray man, another dentist, and—what worried Cherry—a specialized nurse-anaesthetist. The anaesthetist was the most important of the three, and Major Pierce had told Cherry that this special nurse would be flown to the jungle as soon as possible. The other two would follow the unit whenever Army guides next made this trip.

They started marching. Soon the roads and huts of Port Janeway were behind them, then the bare dirt plateau was left behind. One by one, in single file, following the Army men who guided them, the brown-clad figures slid down a crumbling coral hill and entered the thick tangle of jungle.

It was almost dark in here, damp and sweetish, with tropical trees and vines so thickly overgrown that the sun never penetrated. Cherry led the column of nurses. They moved down a narrow trail, advancing with painful slowness, pushing aside huge fantastic leaves, clinging to tough roots while they slid down the bank of a stream, crouching to avoid a bush which turned out to be only a strange pattern of shadows. There was a deathly hush. It was a relief to know that at least there were no Jap snipers in these palms. But birds and animals and snakes hid in this undergrowth, watching, listening.

Cherry looked back at her nurses. The girls' faces, mottled in the dim greenish half-light, were frightened.

"This is it!" she called out cheerfully. "We're really on our way to what we've been training for!" Her voice echoed and died in the tense stillness.

Behind her came Vivian Warren's plaintive voice. "Nursing in the jungle—it's an impossible assignment! How can we ever do it? How can we ever get through this maze to set up our hospital?" Other discouraged voices echoed her.

"We'll do it," Cherry called grimly. "We have to, and we will. Come on!"

The trail rose abruptly and they struggled, single file, up a muddy incline. Far back on the line, Cherry heard a splash. Word was relayed up to her, "Josie Franklin fell in the stream." The girls could not help giggling.

"Anyone else dunked?" Cherry called out, sounding gay. "Will you kindly count noses?"

The giggles spread down the line. The report "All noses are accounted for!" was quickly relayed to Cherry, and she led them off again.

At midday they paused for food and rest. Then they wormed their way still deeper into the jungle. That night they bivouacked and slept on bedrolls beside a river.

Late the next morning they came to a clearing. Smoke from fires, then tents and an American flag, hove into view. Cherry felt a great tug of happiness. The first outpost! Those young infantrymen in worn green fatigues—gaunt, bearded, toughened young soldiers— were the ones she had trained to help, and now she had actually reached them!

"Girls!" the young men cried in disbelief. "Never mind the pants and helmets—they're American girls! What are you girls doing wandering around in the jungle?"

"We're nurses!" Cherry replied proudly. And the young men cheered them.

Cherry was so busy getting her own section set up here that she only half-noticed the other two sections of the medical unit march away, after a brief rest, under the commands of Major Pierce and of Colonel Pillsbee's aide. Colonel Pillsbee himself remained with Cherry's section. The medical tents and equipment were quickly unpacked by corpsmen. The tents, big and little, went up so fast it reminded Cherry of a traveling circus playing a one-day stand back home.

Then both sick and well soldiers slowly filtered into the medical tents. They were young men, but their faces showed the strain of war. Most of them had seen battle action. Now they had been sent back here, temporarily, to do some much-needed work. Cherry saw various equipment—they might have been building an air strip, or manning long-range artillery and anti-aircraft, or clearing the jungle for transportation later on, or doing communications work. But whatever it was, many of these men showed exhaustion. Some wore bandages, where their own medical officer had given first aid.

As Cherry went from tent to tent, supervising her nurses and seeing that the doctors had everything they needed, the soldiers were stoically silent. Not one complained. A few had old, aching battle wounds. Twice as many had ordinary medical conditions, cuts and infections, and tropical ailments. All bore marks of a terrible struggle with the jungle.

"They not only have to fight the Japs," Cherry reflected, "they have to fight this wild, disease-laden jungle as well! But, at least, we can help them!" When she remembered that these uncomplaining young men had said good-by to their families, given up promising careers in midstream, left safe comfortable homes to protect the rest of us, she thought, "Why, if we weren't here to help them, it would be like—like abandoning them!"

None of the nurses complained, as they worked hard and long in those tents. Cherry worked hard, too, keeping things running smoothly, doing a difficult dressing when Mai Lee asked for help, bringing in medicines and vitamin capsules to leave behind for these men.

Another person who was everywhere, poking his nose into everything, was Commanding Officer Pillsbee. He stalked about on his short legs like a sawed-off stork, not adding a bit to Cherry's self-confidence. She was already shaky about this brand-new executive duty. The stern realities of this camp certainly constituted her first test.

"I'm darned if I'm going to get grim about it," Cherry told herself. "A good laugh never hurt anyone."

All day she remembered to smile, to give her nurses not only instructions but a cheering word, and to brace the men by joking with them. The soldiers wanted sympathy but they would have been offended if Cherry had said, "You poor boy, let me take care of that arm," or, "My, I'm sorry. You're wonderfully brave." But Cherry said, "Come over here, hero, let's see if you're brave enough to have that burn cleaned and dressed," and they loved it.

"You medics are always pestering us," the soldiers grouched good-naturedly, as Cherry lined them up before the doctors' tent for a quick checkup.

"You're next, soldier," Cherry teased in another tent. "Now let the nurse hold your hand," as a smiling Ann came up to take a fever-ridden soldier's pulse and respiration. The soldier smiled wanly and almost affectionately in reply.

"You're going to be fine and dandy," Cherry told a hollow-eyed youngster, and gave him a friendly pat on the shoulder. "Honestly you are." He looked so comforted that Cherry could have cried.

There was no doubt about it, the girls' friendly smiles and warm-hearted encouragement were doing these tense, strained, half-forgotten infantrymen as much good as the medicines and treatments. Even the unit doctors commented on it.

Only Colonel Pillsbee disagreed. At suppertime when Cherry reported to headquarters, he raised his small, beady eyes from a map, and said:

"Lieutenant Ames, I would suggest that your nurses behave with a little more—er—formality. A little less, shall I say, a little less levity."

Cherry's mouth fell open. "The nurses are only being kind and friendly, sir!"

"I don't understand what all the laughing is about," Colonel Pillsbee puzzled.

"No," Cherry thought in sudden realization, "you don't understand laughter, do you? You understand responsibility and duty, luckily for the rest of us, but not laughter." She was almost sorry for him. Aloud she said, "We're *trying* to make the patients laugh and feel cheerful, sir. We feel it helps them to get well."

He blinked his eyes at her. "Ah, yes. Of course I approve of your helping your patients to recover." But Colonel Pillsbee was inflexible. "Aren't your nurses being a bit—er—forward? Couldn't their cheerfulness be a trifle more restrained?"

Cherry sighed hopelessly. "Yes, sir." Colonel Pillsbee was a good and well-meaning man, she saw, but he was an iron-clad disciplinarian of the old school. Youth and high spirits had no place in the stiffly conscientious rules he lived by.

"As for your own behavior," Colonel Pillsbee cocked his head at Cherry in his birdlike fashion, "you are the leader and your behavior should be exemplary."

"But, sir, what did I do that was wrong?" Cherry felt her cheeks flaming redder than ever.

Colonel Pillsbee said disapprovingly, "Your laughter sounded to me—I believe the right words are, a little too flippant. A little more dignity and formality, Lieutenant Ames."

"Yes, sir," she muttered. It was useless to try to explain to him. "Here is my report of the day's work, sir.

We plan to work tonight, also. Will that be all, Colonel Pillsbee?"

"Yes, thank you, Lieutenant Ames. Have your nurses on the road at eight-thirty tomorrow morning, with all equipment packed. And I do not mean eight-thirty-one."

"Yes, sir." He dismissed Cherry, and she left, shaking her head.

Several of the girls were waiting for her under a tree. They had saved her her supper from the cook tent, and were keeping it warm under a helmet. When they saw Cherry's dismayed face, they demanded:

"What did The Pill say to you?"

"You mean Mr. Sourpuss!"

"I guess we mean Colonel Icicle."

Cherry sat down cross-legged beside them, and reached for her mess gear. "Never mind, little pitchers. You kids have outsize ears." She was not going to relay Colonel Pillsbee's "formality" order until she discussed it with the unit director. Cherry was reasonably sure that Major Pierce would not give them any such misguided order.

The tropical sky burned and suddenly darkened, as the girls spent their supper hour under the tree. Their talk turned to home.

"Boy, when this war is over," Gwen declared, "I'm never going any farther than the corner drugstore! I'll just stay in our mining town, where my Dad's the doctor, and be his nurse."

"You know what I'm homesick for?" Marie Swift said thoughtfully. Marie was a small, blonde girl, who found nursing more thrilling than anything her wealth had ever bought her. "I miss Spencer most of all!"

The girls' thoughts turned to the great white hospital where they had had their nurses' training. "Golly, we had fun there," Vivian Warren said, laughing reminiscently. "Wonder if the student nurses there now have such a picnic?"

"Did you ever hear of a student nurse who *didn't* have fun?" Cherry countered. "What I'm wondering is how many smart girls are taking advantage of that nursing education provided by the Government."

"I just love the gray Cadet uniform," Mai Lee said dreamily.

"*I* just love—" Cherry said, and started to fish in her big patch pockets. She always carried her letters with her. "You kids remember Mildred Burnham, the probationer I 'adopted.' Well, she's a senior now. She'd only be a junior, except that she transferred to the U.S. Cadet Nurse Corps in the middle of her training."

"Huh!" said Bertha. "Instead of three years in nursing school, only two and a half years in school, and six months' real practical experience with some Federal agency! That's *something!*"

"It's funny," Cherry mused. "Mildred is a very good but not spectacular student, and her parents could afford to pay for her training. But here the Government is paying her whole nursing school tuition, plus her living expenses, plus an allowance, plus—"she grinned at Mai Lee "—that stunning gray uniform. If Mildred can qualify for the Cadet Nurse Corps, I should think lots of other smart girls could, too. They could even enter training direct from high school. Well, anyhow, here's Mildred's letter."

Cherry opened the crumpled sheet. The sun had already set, since they were just south of the equator, and she read aloud by flashlight. Mildred had written:

"Here's what I'm going to do when I graduate—ahem! I'm going to repay the Cadet Nurse Corps by giving six months' nursing to the Government. Old Undecided (that's me) still doesn't know whether she'll volunteer for civilian nursing or Army nursing. I've received so many offers of jobs, my head is spinning. I guess a nurse is never out of work. In the meantime, it's scrumptious being a senior!"

"A senior!" Marie Swift groaned. "Now you've really made me homesick for Spencer!"

The girls were quiet, thinking, remembering.

"What I'm homesick for," Vivian winked hugely at Cherry, "is one of those mysteries you specialize in."

"Oh, we won't find any mysteries out here," Cherry scoffed. "Plenty of insects and fever, but no mysteries."

"Don't say that so fast!" Ann sat up one one elbow. "Nurses are always coming across medical mysteries and—and——"

"Strange wounds," Gwen supplied eagerly. "Remember that case in the newspapers recently, where a man was found to be a spy because a strange bullet burn on his hand gave him away?"

"How about our portable X-ray?" Marie Swift offered. "Or the unit's diathermy machine? You could flash short-wave signals with those!"

"My gosh, what notions you ladies have!" Cherry laughed. "Well, here's hoping you find a mystery. I know I don't expect to. *Oh!*" she exclaimed, as she glanced down at her watch. "Seven o'clock—and there's lots to be done yet."

The girls scrambled to their feet and hurried back to work.

Electric lights, belonging to the work battalion here, had been strung across trees and through tents. In the operating tent, the power was working. An operating table made of planks set upon sawhorses was set up. Captain Bennett, a surgeon, was preparing to operate on an emergency appendicitis case in this crude but sanitary tent. Cherry assigned one of her nurses as anaesthetist to aid the surgeon. She herself worked as operating nurse. After that, she checked on the work of all her other nurses. By midnight Cherry ached all over with fatigue. Almost everyone was asleep, except the sentries and conscientious Colonel Pillsbee, when Cherry still sat making out her night report by the light of a lantern. At last she crawled into the pup tent she shared with Gwen.

"A-a-a-h!" Gwen greeted her, and went right back to sleep.

Next morning the nurses were on the road at eight-thirty, "and not eight-thirty-one," Cherry thought, breathless but triumphant. The medical tents had magically turned into big bundles on the corpsmen's shoulders. Grateful soldiers waved good-by as the little band started off.

That day and the next were, as Ann said, "More of the same, only more so." Pushing with slow difficulty all day through the silent, winding jungle, at evening they arrived at the next outpost to rejoin the second section of the unit. They camped overnight, pushed on again in the morning. By midmorning, the whole unit was together again.

Major Pierce congratulated Cherry. "Your leapfrog plan worked out as neatly as a hole in one," he laughed. Cherry glowed at her unit director's praise.

"You know, Major Pierce, we thought this assignment was impossible," she confessed. "But we've done it!"

"Sure you did it," Major Pierce said, an amused twinkle on his attractive face. "But if you nurses think this was difficult, then, in those classic words, 'you ain't seen nothing yet!'"

Cherry's excitement mounted at Major Pierce's prediction, and at approaching so close now to their destination. The final lap of their trek turned out to be the hardest. The last outpost sent them part of the way, over a grassy plain, in two-and-a-half ton Army trucks. Cherry gasped, as she bounced in the truck, "If this is—riding, I'll—oops!—walk!" But when the terrain grew so muddy and rutted that the trucks could no longer get through, and everyone took to his own two feet, even riding in a broken-down wheelbarrow would have been acceptable.

Laborious hours under heavy pack and through scratchy foliage brought groans, moans, and the nurses' first real complaints. By afternoon, the girls were very tired, and Cherry realized that their spirits drooped along with their bodies.

"Onward, my sissies!" she called back to the long column she led. "It's only about a million miles more!"

"I'll bet we're marching all the way to Asia!" someone shouted unhappily.

From farther back, Mai Lee lifted her quiet voice. "If we're ever anywhere near Asia," the little Chinese-American girl called, "there's a certain village where I have work to do." Cherry and the girls fell silent. They knew Mai Lee meant her family's peaceful ancestral little town, which the Japs had destroyed.

Cherry saw that this turn of the conversation was depressing the girls still more. Footsteps lagged. In desperation, Cherry suggested, "Let's sing," and started rather quaveringly herself.

Vivian, the rather wistful girl Cherry had helped through a misguided romance, loyally joined in. Gwen made the duet a trio. "The rest of us will have to sing, if only to drown you three out," Ann sighed, poked Marie, and they joined the chorus. Presently other girls sang too. Before long the whole column was singing. The steady rhythm, the heartening tunes, gave them a feeling of being warmly together and the remainder of the journey seemed less arduous.

Finally they came to a beach. At the water's edge, Cherry and her nurses halted. This was the farthest tip of Janeway Island. They had reached the jumping-off point. Ahead stretched only blue sky and blue water. The far-off guns were louder here.

Colonel Pillsbee herded the big unit into the many Higgins boats, manned by Marines, waiting on the beach. Cherry and most of her nurses seated themselves in close formation in one boat, some of the nurses sat with corpsmen in another. These were square, stubby, wooden boats, with a front wall that dropped down for a gangplank. Cherry declared they all looked like so many bundles of groceries packed tightly in a square grocery box. Sitting down like this, their heads came neatly to the top of the boat walls, so they could see exactly nothing, nothing but blazing blue sky over them. Just when they were bursting with curiosity!

Suddenly the boats roared, rapidly turned around, and they were skimming across the water—headed like swift sea birds for Pacific Island 14.

CHAPTER III

Island 14

CHERRY STOOD UP IN THE BOAT. RISING OUT OF THE tropic sea were three islands, fringed with tall palms and ablaze with flowers. Their boats sped toward the center island. From this distance, it looked to Cherry like a giant ant hill, with crawling movement everywhere. Nearer, she made out men in green fatigues working up and down the long beach.

The Higgins boats crawled right up on the sand. The girls jumped off and blinked in the intense sun and heat. Cherry did not know where to look first.

Seabees, the sailor-workmen, carried boxes of supplies on their shoulders. Other Seabees were hammering away on a half-finished wooden building under the trees. Engineers drove a noisy bulldozer, laying down rough roads. A big stout man, apparently a beachmaster, roared orders. Cherry's trained eyes picked out several camouflaged fortifications.

What really made her catch her breath were signs of recent battle. In hollow ground stood a heavy mortar, the gun camouflaged with a net roof of leaves. She saw half a grass hut standing, the other half crumpled on the ground, sliced neatly away by a shell. She stood there and stared at the mute evidence of war that lay all around her.

Major Pierce and another officer, in green fatigues, came up the beach to the waiting nurses. "I think the first thing the unit had better do," Major Pierce called out, "is get acquainted with the place. This is Captain May, the Intelligence Officer. Captain May's head-quarters, called G–2, is on Island 13, but you will see him around here on 14 once or twice a week. Captain May is going to take us on a tour and explain things."

The Intelligence Officer nodded pleasantly to the medical people, who gathered around. He was a very young man, self-contained and average-looking, except for his extraordinarily alert eyes. Cherry liked the friendly, informal way he talked to them.

"Well, I'll start at the beginning. Only about three weeks ago, these three small islands were the scene of combat. We took them from the Japs. That was the gun-fire you heard on Janeway. Our troops are fighting on, trying to seize more islands to the northwest. That's the gunfire you'll hear occasionally on Island 14. We may be bombed," he warned. "The Japs haven't bombed for a long time, they must be saving up for something. Or our troops on the forward islands are keeping them too busy. You can't see those islands, but they're only thirty miles from here. So you see," Captain May turned to the nurses, "you young women are as close to the fighting as the Army lets its nurses go."

Cherry spoke up, "If we were in a field hospital, we could go within six miles of combat, couldn't we?"

Captain May smiled. "Yes, in an emergency. But this ought to be dangerous enough to satisfy anybody. The Japs may make an attempt to retake these islands, or as I said before, they may bomb us. That is why we black-out every night."

The medical unit listened with visible excitement. Captain May gave them a sharp look, and resumed, "As soon as Islands 13, 14, and 15 were ours, the Seabees and the Engineers came in. Three weeks ago this place was a wilderness. The Japs never make their islands habitable. Their troops live under the most primitive conditions—they built only some pillboxes. There was nothing at all here but jungle. Now—well, you'll see!"

Jeeps and trucks rolled up. The entire unit climbed in and followed the Intelligence Officer's jeep all around the island. Here, to their amazement, they found a small community hacked out of the jungle. There was a power plant, there were roads, electric lights strung on palm trees, running water for washing, and hanging on trees were Lister bags holding purified water for drinking. Cherry saw mesh hammocks suspended between palm trees in a grove where the Seabees slept, many hammocks but scattered for security, with foxholes dug directly underneath. They passed a column of infantrymen, who, despite the heat, wore heavy clothes and even gloves for protection against disease-bearing insects. The soldiers looked up in amazement and waved joyously when the jeeps full of girls passed.

"Now try to get this picture clear in your minds," Captain May called to them. The jeeps and trucks halted in a sand cay and formed a circle at his signal. "This island is roughly oval in shape. Your hospital will be in the center, for secrecy and for safety. To protect you and your hundreds of patients, there are, scattered over this island, an Infantry Division—that's three Infantry regiments; one regiment of Artillery; and an Antiaircraft detachment. That's mighty good protection.

"Working with these riflemen and heavy gunners," the Intelligence Officer continued, "are a Signal Corps company for communications; a Quartermaster company for supplies; and one platoon of Military Police. The Seabees, the workmen you saw on the beach, will be leaving soon, their work is almost finished. Colonel Pillsbee"—Cherry sighed at the name—"is in charge of everybody and everything. And then there's one other thing——"

The Intelligence Officer hesitated and frowned. He held a whispered consultation with Major Pierce, seemingly doubtful about something. Finally, he turned to the medical people again.

"I am going to entrust you with some confidential information. You will see and hear certain activities going on, especially at night. You might as well know what they are—so you won't be tempted to write anything in your letters home about this. Let me warn you that this is a closely guarded operation."

Cherry and the other girls looked at one another. What was up?

Captain May pointed to the northern tip of their island. "Up there you will see Army Air Forces men unrolling steel mesh mats on the sand. Those are for plane runways. *They are building a secret air base here.* Short-range fighter planes will refuel here. Also, in order to supply our troops fighting up forward—and perhaps ourselves in case of emergency—Air Transport Command supply planes will land here at this halfway base."

"Air Transport Command!" Cherry breathed to Ann and Gwen, beside her in the jeep. "That's where my brother Charlie is now!"

She was so excited she hardly heard the rest of the Intelligence Officer's remarks. Charlie might conceivably fly here! Cherry hoped hard that he would. And then she remembered the watchful enemy only thirty miles away, and she hoped just as hard that Charlie would not be flying into range of those enemy guns. It never occurred to her to be afraid for herself.

When the unit returned to the center of camp late in the afternoon, Cherry thought every soldier on the island must have hiked over to greet them. Young, lanky, casual, thin shoulders bent under heavy rifles, dirty worn fatigues and caked mud on their heavy shoes, but wide smiles on their drawn, tired faces. As the nurses climbed down from the jeeps and trucks, the soldiers surged forward. The Army rule forbidding enlisted men and nurses, who are officers, to fraternize, was momentarily laid aside as the soldiers cried out:

"Girls! Real live American girls! Gosh, are we glad to see you!"

"You're the first American women we've seen in two years! Any of you nurses from Red Oaks, Kansas?"

"Girls from home! Nurses! And we thought Headquarters had picked us to be the Forgotten Men!"

"This is almost as good as having my mother show up!"

One of the soldiers seized Cherry's hand and shook it. Every face she looked at was stunned and overjoyed. Cherry swallowed hard. So they had been cut off for two monotonous years in the nightmare jungle! These fighting men looked to her suspiciously like homesick small boys. They were pathetically eager for the nurses to make some sort of response.

Cherry impulsively stepped forward. "We're just as glad to see you as you are to see us! We're going to take good care of you! And—and—" She looked into the waiting, lonesome faces, and was so moved she forgot such things as rules "—and you're all invited to a party! The nurses invite the whole island to a party!"

This time, her sixty nurses as well as the crowd of soldiers let out a delighted yell. General bedlam and joy broke loose. "A party!" "Oh, boy!" "We haven't had any fun in months!"

"With refreshments!" Cherry shouted over the uproar.

"Ice cream?" several very young boys shouted back eagerly. "We sure do miss ice cream!"

"And ice cream," Cherry promised blindly. "And entertainment!" she added in a shout. She could not stop herself. She impulsively promised, and the next moment wondered desperately how she could keep her promises. Well, she would make good on her promises if she got court-martialed for it!

At that moment, Colonel Pillsbee's aide came hurrying down a little hill and approached Cherry. "The Commanding Officer wishes to speak to Lieutenant Ames!"

The soldiers scattered to their posts. Major Pierce rather hastily led the nurses away. Cherry was left alone to accompany the furiously silent aide up the hill.

The command tent and Colonel Pillsbee's tent quarters had just been set up on a high cleared plot of ground, and some soldiers were building a wooden railing to enclose Headquarters. "Colonel Pillsbee *would* erect a railing between himself and the rest of us," Cherry thought. That railing made her feel quakingly as if she were entering a jail, instead of the headquarters tent.

"What is this talk of parties?" Colonel Pillsbee demanded primly.

Cherry stood before him and explained, or at least she did her best to explain.

"Don't you know the nurses are not to mingle socially with the enlisted men?" Colonel Pillsbee reproved her.

"Yes, sir, but this is a group party," Cherry sought for tactful words. "The girls won't be having dates, sir, they'll just be acting as—well, sir, as Army hostesses to several regiments."

Colonel Pillsbee considered this. The good Army word "regiments" and the phrase "Army hostesses" had an impersonal, formal ring; they satisfied him. "But," the Commanding Officer said, his small eyes like chips of ice, "these men are fighting men. We must not coddle them. It softens them, and does them real harm when they have to face combat."

Cherry thought anxiously that Colonel Pillsbee had an indisputable point there. Then she thought of those homesick faces. "Would just *one* party do them very much harm?" she pleaded. "After all, sir, these men have been stationed on islands like these for two years, and it seems, at least to me, sir," she said gingerly and very respectfully, "that their morale is a little— discouraged."

Colonel Pillsbee in his turn looked anxious. "Sit down, Lieutenant Ames." Cherry sat down on the edge of a box, scarcely daring to breathe.

"Two years here is a long time," Colonel Pillsbee admitted. A shadow crossed his face. Cherry realized that in his touch-me-not way, he cared deeply for his men.

"Well, Lieutenant Ames, suppose I gave permission. How would you propose to manage a party of that size, and furnish the ice cream and entertainment which I heard you indiscreetly promise?"

He was now at least considering the idea! "I haven't the slightest idea where I'll get those things, sir," Cherry replied blithely, "but I'll find them! I won't let those men down!"

Colonel Pillsbee tapped a bony finger on his table. "I am opposed to this party. It sets a bad precedent. One thing leads to another—I fail to see the need for such a display of sentiment. If the men need relaxation, we will arrange something more suitable. For example, a swimming hour every day."

Cherry's hopes sank. "But, Colonel Pillsbee, I promised the men! I can't go back on my word!"

"That," the Commanding Officer observed coldly, "is the only reason I am troubling to discuss this matter with you, Lieutenant Ames. Ordinarily, I would summarily refuse permission. But an officer's word is his bond, and you have—most impertinently, I must say—pledged your word. I cannot afford to sacrifice the confidence of the personnel in their Chief Nurse. Therefore——"

"Oh, thank you, sir!"

Colonel Pillsbee looked at her. His face stiffened. "Lieutenant Ames, I strongly disapprove of this party and of your behavior. From now on, you will not undertake matters pertaining to general personnel without consulting your Commanding Officer first."

"I—I'm sorry, sir," Cherry faltered. She got to her feet, feeling humiliated and scared. But she had won permission for their party!

"One more thing, Lieutenant Ames. You may not have this party until the hospital is completely set up."

"Yes, sir." It meant a wait but of course he was right. Cherry dared one glance at Colonel Pillsbee's frozen face. "Thank you, sir," she said, saluted, and fled.

Hurrying down the hill, she lectured herself. "Ames, be careful! You're only *acting* Chief Nurse. You must turn in such a bang-up job, and be such a goody-goody, that the C.O. will *have* to approve of you!"

Setting up a hospital on this South Sea island was a big order, and a large part of it was up to Cherry and her nurses. It had to be done swiftly, too. The advance detail had brought in a great deal of equipment, sorted it out, and set up a few tents temporarily. Now Major Pierce chose a treeless clearing in the heart of the island, as a sort of yard and traffic center. Around that open oblong of ground, the corpsmen set up tents under the high concealing palm trees.

At one end of the open yard was the Medical Headquarters tent, with Major Pierce's and Cherry's offices, and the Receiving tent for new cases. In back of these was the doctors' quarters. At the opposite end of the yard, the Seabees built them a supply shed, and in back of that was the nurses' quarters. Then down one long side of the clearing, they set up an Operating Room in a portable Quonset hut, and flanked the O.R. by three smaller tents, one for X-ray and laboratory work, one for dispensary and pharmacy, and one for dental. Along the other long side of the yard were diet kitchens and the unit's mess hall, and beside it a shack which Cherry hoped to turn into a recreation room. Then, all around this nerve-center, the various wards—medical, surgical, orthopedic, contagious; several of each—were laid out in big tents and thatched pavilions. Finally, enclosing the whole hospital grounds like a ring, came quarters for the two hundred corpsmen. A weird city of canvas mushroomed in a week.

Cherry wished they could have streets and gardens to take away the bare utilitarian look of the place. But there were more essential things to attend to first, like tacking up screens and netting against dangerous insects; working out how to camouflage and still admit sunlight for their patients; and furnishing the rough wards. There was not very much with which to make a thousand-bed hospital: a few hundred white iron hospital beds with not very comfortable mattresses, many Army cots and thin mattresses, some crude wooden two-decker beds draped with nets, not nearly enough tables and supply cabinets. Cherry and her nurses, even with the corpsmen's willing help, had a struggle. But they evolved clean, orderly wards, surprisingly like a hospital at home. Already they had forty patients, with appendicitis, broken bones, and various infections, to admit to their new wards.

An infantryman showed up one day and announced he had been a sign painter in civilian life. He made them neat, businesslike signs reading, "Medical Ward" and "C. Ames, Chief Nurse & Registrar" and "Purified Water" and "Quiet Please Period." The American flag, and beneath it the Red Cross flag, flew from Medical

Headquarters tent, and their hospital began to take on the look of a going concern.

Cherry met many new people in their joint struggle to set up the hospital. Major Pierce was not only unit director but chief surgeon. By this time Cherry already knew the other doctors and technicians by name. Now she met and worked with the Chief Medical Officer, white-haired Captain Jonas, who handled the administrative or non-medical affairs of the unit. Cherry worked with Captain Ricciardi, a plump smiling man, the supply officer, and Captain Penrose, a soldierly man who commanded the corpsmen, and the pharmacist who described himself as "head of the iodine squad." She also met Captain Bill Wilson, a tall young Texan who was mess officer.

Working with these highly trained, experienced men specialists, in these first two weeks, took every ounce of resourcefulness and maturity Cherry possessed. She had to be as efficient as they were, and it was no easy task to measure up to these men.

Busy as she was, Cherry's feminine instincts kept cropping up. She had an overwhelming desire to make this bare place livable and homelike.

So did the other girls. When they had first trooped into Nurses' Quarters, Gwen had given a yelp and dubbed it "The Ritz Stables." It was a long, bare shed with a dirt floor. Cherry, though Chief Nurse, was squeezed in there with the rest of the girls. The nurses had cots and Army blankets, and not another thing. "What we need is a note of luxury," Gwen declared desperately. Now that their work on the hospital was well under way, the girls determined to do something about their quarters.

"Something drastic, please," Ann said. "The only thing you can say for our palatial abode is that you can't get lonesome in here."

For besides sixty nurses, the small shed was jammed with footlockers, framed photographs and piles of uniforms. Shelves overflowed with cold cream jars, shoes, and water buckets. Everything was draped with that troublesome mosquito netting. The girls constantly tripped over things and one another. Cherry appointed a Housekeeping Committee.

"First," said Bertha Larsen, "we'll give our Ritz Stables a good cleaning."

There was no soap to spare. Marie Swift confessed she had been hoarding some scented soap. So they moved cots and footlockers and clothing out into the sun, and scrubbed the walls and shelves and rafters with Marie's best "Blue Carnation." The hose, extra buckets, and broom were tactfully stolen from the G.I.'s by Gwen, and later returned. On their off-duty hours, all the nurses pitched in to cover the dirt floor with bamboo, over which they laid fresh-smelling eucalyptus bark.

Many of the girls had brought colorful, sturdy bed-spreads with them. Cherry devised black-out curtains—they had been groping around in the dark at night, and stout curtains meant they could have lights indoors, even with distant guns rumbling. Cherry persuaded two dozen nurses to contribute spare bath towels, including her own, cut them down to uniform size, and then Bertha tinted them green, with a home-made grass dye she knew how to brew. Pictures, and one particularly nice bedspread went up on the rough wood walls. Ann, who had green fingers, gathered flame flowers and transplanted them beside the door and path. The Ritz Stables fully deserved its name.

But most satisfying of all was the nursing. So far, the original forty patients had swelled only to fifty. Cherry assigned nurses to these patients, and the rest of the girls completed setting up the hospital. It was strange to see nurses on the crude wards, not in the usual crisp white, or even Army seersucker, but wearing their olive drab trousers, blouses and helmets. To the sick men, they looked wonderful. "Gosh!" the soldiers said. "White sheets and American girls!" When Cherry marched her nurses past the rows of soldiers' tent barracks, the men would come out and stand at smiling attention to honor them.

"As long as we're playing house," Cherry said briskly to her nurses, soon after they had fixed up the Ritz

Stables, "what about fixing up the spare shed next to Mess Hall for a clubroom for the others?" This time she was careful to secure Colonel Pillsbee's permission first. They gave that shed, too, a good scrubbing, a floor, and curtains. By that time, word had spread, and soldiers, doctors, and corpsmen all showed up in their free hours, eager to help. The officers were very willing to let their men take part. Half the job here was waiting, with its inevitable boredom. The officers even granted extra free hours, when it was possible, for the men to work on the clubroom.

The soldiers built tables, bookshelves, and chairs of a sort, out of boxes. The departing Seabees presented them with some leftover yellow paint, which promptly went on the clubroom walls and furniture. The girls added all the wild flowers they could find. "It doesn't look bad at all," Major Pierce said, as he hammered away cheerfully at a half-finished ping-pong table. Somebody put up a large poster: *Buy War Bonds!* Finally, the nurses contributed books and magazines, and Cherry lent her radio for the general welfare. The men, not to be outdone, brought to the recreation room more reading matter, games of all sorts, even a small portable victrola and records. Soldier-patients, eager to get up and see it, sent cherished belongings. The clubroom was a real success. The sign painter painted "Seventh Heaven" above the door.

Colonel Pillsbee stepped in once, commented, "There will be no nurses permitted in here, except at special hours for ladies exclusively," and departed. But as long as Colonel Pillsbee was permitting them to have their party, no one minded.

They could have had the party now, for all the essential work was done. But Cherry's homemaking impulse had spread, and everyone wanted to make the island as livable as possible. Cherry was touched at the love of home these men evinced. The Engineers had laid down rough roads, and now the men turned these and the hospital lanes into neat streets. In their spare time, they made narrow borders of coral, leading to the tents, and signs: "Victory Avenue," "World's End Boulevard," and— to Cherry's surprise and pleasure—"Cherry Square." Many of the streets were named after nurses. Major Pierce had a popular idea: he detailed some of the corpsmen to lay out a baseball field. "It will be good exercise for healing muscles," he told his Chief Nurse, "and besides, I pitch a pretty mean ball myself!" Ann had a good idea, too. One of her patients had received packets of seeds from home, so Ann encouraged her ambulatory patients to plant and tend a garden. They planted marigolds, poppies, morning-glory vines, as well as vegetables, to add to their tinned and dried rations.

Now Cherry began to think about providing the ice cream and entertainment she had promised.

"Refreshments first!" the girls voted. Cherry went to consult the mess officer.

"Ice cream?" Captain Wilson echoed, and looked at Cherry as if she had gone mad. "Why, there's no ice here, no churn or vacuum. Impossible."

Cherry frowned worriedly. But she was determined to find a way to keep her promise and supply the ice cream. It was amazing how much the men craved ice cream, more than any other food except candy.

"Cheer up," the nurses told her, "we'll all chip in our candy bars."

"That's not much for all these men," Cherry worried.

Josie Franklin piped up. "Why don't you see Miltie Fruitcake?"

Cherry found her way to a private called Milton who did indeed have several fruitcakes.

"Yes, ma'am, you've very welcome to them," he said. "That's the only kind of cake my wife can send me that will keep, and she certainly keeps on sending them. Five pounds at a time. Several other men have wives like mine. In fact, Lieutenant Ames, this island is going to sink some day under the weight of fruitcakes. If you like, I could collect them for you."

Private Milton contributed his own three fruitcakes, and collected thirty-three more for Cherry. That made nearly two hundred pounds of fruitcake. Ann suggested a cool drink made of coconut milk and chocolate malt—there was an excess supply of chocolate malt on hand, for some reason. Bertha, out of her farm experience, suggested a sort of fruitade made from the berries and sweet fruits that grew lushly here. They could chill it all the day before in the deep stream. And the mess officer turned up with two gross boxes of candy bars and some exciting news.

A lone fighter plane, belonging to an aircraft carrier, had made a forced landing on their half-finished air base. Unable to radio either his carrier or Island 14 in advance, because the enemy might hear his radio message, the fighter pilot had simply landed. He would have to stay here a few days, Captain Wilson said, and told Cherry, "So now you will have your ice cream."

"I don't see the connection between a stranded fighter plane and making ice cream," Cherry puzzled.

"Simple," Captain Wilson assured her, laughing. "Fighter planes go up almost into the stratosphere, thirty thousand feet up, where the temperature is far below zero. Why, up there, you can freeze ice cream in half an hour!"

"But—but—you can't load a fighter plane with *ice cream*," Cherry sputtered.

"If you can load it with four hundred pounds of ammunition, you could just as easily load it with four hundred quarts of ice cream. Let's see, you'll need about eight hundred quarts—that's two half-hour trips——"

"But what officer is ever going to authorize such a thing?" Cherry asked unbelievingly.

"The morale officer has already convinced Colonel Pillsbee to authorize it," Captain Wilson replied with a broad grin.

"And you convinced the morale officer, first! Captain Wilson, you—you're a real friend!"

The young Texan touched his cap in salute and turned away, calling back over his shoulder, "Remember to give me a double portion, won't you?"

As for finding the promised entertainment, Cherry had no trouble. So many would-be entertainers deluged her with offers that she had to appoint an Entertainment Committee to hold tryouts and rehearsals. Finally a worn but satisfied Committee notified Cherry they had selected: a very funny mimic who had been a professional actor, a trio of singers with a guitarist, a former artist who promised to do lightning charcoal portraits, the "Iron Man" of the Infantry Division who would do feats of strength, and a good amateur magician. Besides, two nurses, sisters, offered songs and tap dances, and Mai Lee was coaxed to promise some Chinese ceremonial dances in her beautiful robe, which she had brought in her footlocker. Major Pierce was arranging to have a baseball game and a ping-pong match.

Everything was ready now. Cherry went up the hill to see Colonel Pillsbee.

His yellow thatch of hair reminded Cherry more than ever of a bird's topknot, as she cautiously outlined the party's program. But the topnot nodded at each item Cherry named. When she finished, there was not a single thing the Commanding Officer had objected to. "He must have resigned himself," Cherry thought in amazement. Or perhaps Major Pierce, or the other officers, had persuaded him that this "sentimenal nonsense" was really a morale builder.

Colonel Pillsbee said primly, "Very well, Lieutenant Ames. Here are my orders. For reasons of security, this must be a daylight party. Not more than twenty per cent of any detail, including your nurses, and excepting yourself, may leave duty for the party at the same time. That is, you all will attend the party in relays for an hour at a time. Your party will therefore run from twelve noon to five P.M. All the men must be back in their own areas in time for five-thirty mess. Is that clear?"

Cherry wanted to ask, "What about the entertainers? And the baseball teams?" But Colonel Pillsbee had issued an order. She would simply have to hurry up and find more entertainers, more baseball players.

Cherry also wanted to say to Colonel Pillsbee, who after all was permitting them to have a party, "I hope you'll come to our party too, sir." But she was not sure lieutenants could issue invitations to colonels. He would probably come anyway, "to make sure we aren't too frivolous," Cherry thought, as he dismissed her.

When the great day dawned, the nurses worked like beavers. They rushed about their hospital duties, finished last-minute party arrangements, and got ready every patient who could be moved to attend the party too.

At noon, the first soldiers marched into the hospital yard, exactly on time. They were laughing and joking so much Cherry whispered to Ann, "They're in such good spirits that, even if the entertainment goes sour and our refreshments don't quite go around, they'll have fun anyhow!"

But the entertainment was wildly acclaimed, and the supply of ice cream, cake, candy and cool drinks promised to hold out. When the first guests departed, singing, and the next swarm of soldiers marched in under the broiling one o'clock sun, all smiles, Cherry breathed easier. The party was a success!

By late that afternoon, she was limping with fatigue, and her head spun with the talk and laughter, the continuous entertainment on a big table under a tree which served as the stage, victrola records playing in the clubroom, the click of ping-pong balls, and shouts from the baseball diamond. But the whole island had come to the nurses' party! Even Captain May, the Intelligence Officer, and several of his men had come over from Island 13. And Cherry glimpsed Colonel Pillsbee, between Major Pierce and white-haired Captain Jonas, obviously enjoying his portion of ice cream.

That night, after the debris of the party had been cleaned up and all evening ward duty had been completed, the girls collapsed on their cots.

"Wow!" said Gwen, painfully rubbing sunburn lotion on her bright red face. "We sure did have a fine time, all of us!"

"It was worth the work," Ann said faintly, as she and Vivian soaked their aching feet in a bucket of hot water. "It was a gorgeous party!"

Cherry, limp on her cot, opened two drowsy black eyes and grinned at the exhausted nurses. "Well, kids, we've fixed up the hospital, we've made some little civilization on this South Sea island, we gave a get-acquainted party, so now—I guess—Pacific Island 14 is home! And—" she yawned hugely but fought to get out the rest, "—and if we can do this, we can do *anything!*"

CHAPTER IV

~~~~~~

Troubles

BY THE MIDDLE OF FEBRUARY, SPENCER UNIT'S EVACUATION hospital was in full swing. Almost any blazing morning you could find Cherry, wearing Army overalls, in the tent she shared with Major Pierce, seated at her crude table with the folding legs, a folding file and a field telephone in its leather case at her side, her helmet flung on the dirt floor, her black curls tumbled as she worked.

This morning the Chief Nurse was mapping out new ward schedules for her nurses. With at least one nurse, and several corpsmen, needed for each twenty patients, and with their sick list growing, Cherry found there simply were not enough nurses. Where to put whom? And when? Besides, Josie Franklin and Bertha voluntarily been on night duty ever since they arrived in the jungle, and Cherry could not ask them to go through another month of it. Worse, Marie Swift and two other girls were sick, leaving them three nurses short. "The only solution," Cherry scowled, "is to load each girl with forty patients or get more nurses. But there *aren't* more nurses! And there aren't going to be more nurses until more girls become student nurses! Oh-h!"

She labored over the schedules, between interruptions, and turned in despair to the day reports and night reports from the various wards. Then she went on to her duties in the Receiving tent.

Trucks and the unit's two ambulances were pulling up in the glaring sun. Corpsmen unloaded wounded men from the forward islands. Cherry had been hearing occasional, distant gunfire. Here was the result of it. She went into the Receiving tent to talk to Captain Jonas.

"A few wounded," he told her, "but mostly fever and dysentery cases from our own three islands. One man hurt when his jeep rolled over. And an airman stricken at high altitude."

An airman! He must have been landed at the Army Air Forces air base on their island! This was the third mention Cherry had heard of the secret base, the first time when the Intelligence Officer had confidentially told the medical people about it, the second time when the Navy fighter plane was forced down. Did this new arrival mean the air base was completely constructed, finished, now? Did it mean that planes would come to Pacific Island 14 now? But Cherry had heard no planes. She asked Captain Jonas no prying questions, but looked over his records with him. Then she accompanied him down the huge Receiving tent.

Those soldier-patients able to walk went to desks, where Captain Jonas's assistants took their medical histories. Then they turned over all their belongings— barracks bags, worn rifles, mud-covered bayonets. Cherry had to grin when she saw an attendant gingerly accept a hand grenade and give the sick soldier a receipt for it. Behind a flap at the end of the big tent, the soldiers turned in their uniforms and emerged wearing Army hospital pajamas and bathrobes, and their own shoes. Then Cherry stepped in to send the soldiers to the appropriate wards and to notify the ward nurses of their new admissions.

Next, Cherry saw to the mobile services. It still amazed her to see a repair shop in a truck, a laundry on wheels, and a rolling Army kitchen. This last had been wangled from Australia. The nurses had complained to Cherry that food carried on trays from the regular mess kitchen to the distant wards got cold. But now, with this kitchen on wheels, they could bring piping hot food to every patient. The unit even had a portable X-ray and a portable surgical unit for emergencies. Cherry was very proud of all this shiny new equipment and completely fascinated by it. By the time she had talked with the soldier in charge of laundry, arranged to have two stuffed-up ward sinks and an O.R. table repaired, and visited the regular kitchen to order tomorrow's diets, Cherry wished she were on wheels herself.

"An executive shouldn't try to do everything herself!" she sighed, as she started out for the wards and her daily rounds. "I ought to assign Ann to work with Captain Jonas, and Bertha would make a fine dietitian, since our old dietitian was kept on in Panama, and even Josie would be reliable as dispensary nurse. But how can I take them off the wards when we're already short of nurses?" she despaired.

She wished she could talk things over with her old nursing teachers, supervisors and head nurses. Miss Mac or Miss Reamer would know exactly how to help and advise her. She certainly missed these firm, quiet, experienced nurses whom she had loved so much.

On her way to the wards, she groped her way into the darkened X-ray tent. Here films were developed on the spot, for the use of surgeons in the Operating hut. This was a tent within a tent. Major Pierce had received complaints from the surgeons that X-ray was slow and had asked Cherry to "do something about it." She started by asking the two young men in charge of X-ray how their work was going.

"There's something wrong with the machine," they told her. "Oh, we know we're slowing up operations! But we can't help it, Lieutenant Ames—this tube seems to be choked up—we've tried to repair it but no luck—"

Cherry looked at the big, shiny, metal rods, thick rubber tubing, and camera box, sitting incongruously on the dirt floor. She was stumped. The best she could suggest was, "I'll send the repair truck over. And I'll also try to hunt up a soldier who is a mechanic."

Cherry made a note to take care of this and half ran to her next job. She *must* divide up the work—she must have a regular anaesthetist instead of using a ward nurse in O.R.—Just then, she heard a tiny humming above her. Immediately she threw her head back and squinted into the sun. There, high in the brilliant sky, was a plane, looking about as big as a fly. It rapidly crossed their island and proceeded south toward Janeway. Where had it started from?

But there was no time to speculate now. She should have stopped in at the laboratory tent, which overflowed with basins and test tubes and burners. She should have had a look in at the tent drugstore, where hundreds of prescriptions were filled from hundreds of bottles. But there was no time, no time! Cherry scurried on to her daily rounds of the wards.

This was the part Cherry liked best. She missed doing actual nursing, although often enough even the Chief

Nurse was pressed into bedside service. Mostly she missed having patients of her own. However, she knew most of the patients, and they all certainly knew Cherry! She was enormously popular.

"Hello, Lieutenant Ames!" thirty-seven of them called out, as she entered the doorway of Mai Lee's rough Medical Ward.

Cherry grinned and waved and called back to the boys in the beds, "How are you today?" She turned in at the utility room to speak in a low voice to Mai Lee. Mai Lee, with the help of two corpsmen, was setting up trays for the patients' noon dinner. It always reassured Cherry to see standard hospital routine going on here in the jungle, with the same order and cleanliness as in a real hospital back home.

"How are those colds? The shock cases? And the gastritis case?" Cherry asked Mai Lee anxiously.

"Pretty fair," the Chinese-American girl replied. "Come have a look at the charts. But, Cherry, I'm worried about the boy with the brain fever. When Dr. Willard made his eight-thirty sick call this morning, he said we ought to put that boy on isolation and keep him more quiet—if you can possibly arrange a private room for him." Mai Lee's almond eyes pleaded with her.

"Certainly I'll get him a room," Cherry said, hastily scrawling this job too in her tiny notebook. "There isn't any such room but we'll rig one up, that's all. Don't ask me how!" She grinned at Mai Lee. "Anything else?"

"I'm not sure I remember exactly how to set-up for that tricky spinal tap," Mai Lee confessed. "Is this right?"

The two girls carefully recited together the set-up and the difficult technique of assisting the doctor in doing the tap.

"Whew, I sure am glad we studied hard while we were in school," Cherry said. "There's no one here to tell us these things now!"

"Miss Cher-ry!" called a boy's voice. "Aren't you coming in to see us?"

"Sure thing!" and Cherry and Mai Lee went into the ward itself.

Here were the young men who were the whole reason for Cherry's being at this far end of the world. They lay in the none too comfortable cots, tall, lean, limp, sun-burned over their sick pallor, weakly smiling at Cherry and Mai Lee. These bronzed young fighters with the sensitive eyes made special patients from a medical viewpoint. Their irrepressible high spirits and their uncomplaining fortitude made them the most lovable and heroic patients Cherry had ever seen.

Cherry stopped to talk to the blue-eyed boy with the soft Carolina voice.

"How long 'fore I go back and git me some more Japs?" he demanded impatiently.

Did you kill any Japs?" Cherry asked him.

"Oh, yes."

"How?"

"Shootin'."

That was all Carolina would say. But Colorado's strong plain voice came from the next bed.

"Carolina's got three medals."

"Shut yo' mouth," said Carolina, flushing a bright embarrassed red. "I never asked for no medals, Lieutenant Ames."

"Okay, I won't hold the medals against you," Cherry teased, and the whole ward smiled with her.

Cherry walked on slowly, down the row of cots, Mai Lee following her. "This is Private John Andrews, our Chief Nurse," Mai Lee said. "Private Andrews was just admitted with—"

"—with a G.I. haircut," the soldier said in a faint voice. It was one of the boys' favorite jokes. "Hello, ma'am. Are *you* the Chief Nurse?" He started to laugh with pleasure but choked and lay back on the pillow.

"Quiet there, soldier," Cherry murmured, laying a hand on his arm. She knew better than to offer him pity. He looked up at her and grinned.

The soldiers often told the nurses hair-raising stories of their adventures. They had to get it off their chests to someone. They seldom wrote these things home, for fear of worrying their families, because civilians might not understand. But nurses are soldiers, too, and they have their patients' confidence.

There was the man on Postsurgical who had lost a leg. "Well, at least I'm still here," he told Cherry. "Believe me, I'm going to get well and get home some day—because I want to see that boy of mine." He showed her snapshots of the baby son he had not yet seen. Cherry and his own nurse nursed and encouraged him, and he *was* getting better. He would go this very week to Janeway, where a road had been cleared by now, and thence to the base hospital in San Francisco for therapy that would make him active and self-supporting again.

Then there was the quiet soldier who talked and talked to Cherry, trying to clear his fear-struck mind of the unbelievable things that had happened to him. "It's a strange feeling to be hit," he said. "Just a sharp sting, and you don't pay much attention, for you are so intent on your job nothing else seems to matter. But afterwards——"

Afterwards there was the pain. The soldier had managed to take the sulfa powder out of his kit and sprinkle it into his wound to prevent infection. Then litterbearers, searching the field, found him and carried him in. After receiving first aid, a small boat had brought him back here to the evacuation hospital. "It's a good feeling when you're hurt to know the nurses are near by," he said. Cherry had nodded and brought him a deck of cards and a book to cheer him up. She had asked Vivian to watch this soldier's state of mind as well as his physical health. This soldier was discharged from the hospital now, cured, and, he said, "eager to return that bullet!"

There was a cheerful attitude on the wards just the same. Some of Cherry's highly unorthodox but ingenious measures gave the soldiers a lot of laughs. She prescribed nail polish for chigger bites, despite the protests of "Sissy!"—and it worked. She gave a shamming patient a huge pill which he swore "cured" him—the pill consisted of nothing but bicarbonate of soda, to the whole ward's amusement. She ordered fancy foods for soldiers who had no appetites, and they ate out of sheer astonishment. She made a rule that her nurses wear their feminine white uniforms on Sundays and curl their hair and powder their noses, come storms, heat or bombings—and it perked up everybody's morale.

There was a bully on Josie's ward whom timid Josie could not handle. The big, husky soldier roared refusal to take medicine and remained sick, apparently a permanent fixture to haunt Josie. He *had* to take that medicine. This day Cherry decided to challenge his sporting instincts. She held the pill between thumb and forefinger, her black eyes dancing but watchful.

"Now look, Private Edwards." Private Edwards glowered at the pill from his pillow. "I'll toss you for it. If you can catch it, you don't have to take it. If you miss, down your throat it goes!"

The bully grunted. "If *you* miss, you gotta take it."

"All right!" Cherry shot back, while the ward listened eagerly. She flipped the pill.

The pill shot out of Cherry's hand in an arc, flew toward Private Edwards who grabbed and missed it, and rolled merrily along the ward floor. It stopped rolling near the door, and settled before a pair of well-polished boots.

Cherry looked at those boots and gasped. Then slowly, very slowly, she raised her eyes until they were level with Colonel Pillsbee's. "Darn it!" Cherry thought. "Why can't he stay in the military area? Why must he inspect us so often?" But the painstaking Commanding Officer made a daily inspection of the hospital, though it was Major Pierce's job to inspect and then report to Colonel Pillsbee.

"Lieutenant Ames." His voice was very precise, very dry. "I should like to see you outside."

"Yes, sir. Just as soon as I give Private Edwards his pill," Cherry said firmly. She took another pill from the bottle. The bully's mouth was already open in surprise, and the pill went down before he could protest.

Cherry followed the Commanding Officer into the hot, steaming outdoors. But he did not say a word. With his birdlike steps, he started off for the yard, Cherry marching forlornly at his heels. At Medical Headquarters tent, he went in and motioned Cherry to Major Pierce's desk. The three of them sat down together.

"Major Pierce, it is high time we discussed Lieutenant Ames's unseemly conduct," the Commanding Officer started. With the tips of his fingers poised on the desk, Colonel Pillsbee primly outlined the pill incident.

Major Pierce's lips twitched, and he avoided looking directly at Cherry. "The recalcitrant patient took the medicine, though," the unit director pointed out.

Colonel Pillsbee waved a limp hand. "That is beside the point. Lieutenant Ames is—er—almost too popular with the patients. I also do not understand why the nurses must wear white dresses on Sunday. It increases the laundry."

"Very well, Colonel," Major Pierce said, poker face. "Lieutenant Ames will become more dignified and the nurses will cease wearing white dresses."

That left fussy Colonel Pillsbee without much to say. He harumphed and looked at Cherry. "Really, Lieutenant Ames, I cannot help feeling that your youth and good looks are a disadvantage which you must live down. I shall be back tomorrow." Then he stiffly rose and stalked out of the tent.

Cherry and Major Pierce looked at each other and burst out laughing.

"But it's not funny," Cherry said, trying to sober up "The old boy has it in for me. Oh, Major Pierce, how can I make myself older, uglier, and more unpopular?" She went off into another peal of laughter but recovered rather hastily. "Couldn't you please, sir, put in a good word about my work to the Colonel?"

Major Pierce grinned his tough and cheerful grin, but shook his head. "I'm completely satisfied with your work, but this is your problem, young woman. You must solve it yourself—I can't solve it for you." He turned back to the records he was working on.

Cherry felt let-down. She started to leave the tent, wishing for Miss Mac or Miss Reamer or some experienced older woman to guide her. Major Pierce called after her:

"Oh, Lieutenant Ames! Here's a chore for you!"

Cherry came back to his desk. The unit director told her the X-ray had completely broken down and they desperately needed another. He would have to ask the short-wave installation to radio the Air Transport Command to fly in another portable X-ray. Since he could not telephone this confidential message over the camp's general and therefore public line, Major Pierce asked Cherry to go to the short-wave post with this request.

"If we're lucky," he told her, "the anaesthetist might arrive on the same plane with the X-ray."

A plane! An ATC plane coming here to their island! Cherry thought excitedly, "So planes *are* beginning to land at the secret base now!"

But even in her excitement, Cherry could not forget that her troubles with Colonel Pillsbee were growing worse instead of better. She wondered what she could do to square herself. Her work was above reproach, her work was excellent. Colonel Pillsbee had taken a personal dislike to her, that was all. Or maybe—maybe she did not understand *his* viewpoint? Whatever it was, she must find something to do about this, and quickly. If things went on like this, she would find herself relieved of her Chief Nurse's post! And all this put a severe strain on Cherry's idealism. She needed a little understanding and encouragement.

Late that afternoon, Cherry commandeered a jeep and drove to the southern tip of the island, just beyond the Infantry tents. She supposed that she would have to see the Signal Corps men, who handled communications. She wandered over to a group of young men wearing headphones. They were in a three-walled shack, half-hidden in a clump of tall ferns, and worked over a big, folding contraption, a sort of telephone switchboard with plugs and wires.

"You'll have to consult the Intelligence Officer for a radio message," they told her. "We'll telephone over to Island 13 for you."

The signalmen handed Cherry headphones to put on. This was the closed telephone used for confidential messages between Islands 13, 14, and 15, and was also used for code messages to the combat zone up forward. While she waited, she heard these signalmen talking to troops on the embattled forward islands, in a sort of code. It was a curious experience.

Presently she heard Captain May's pleasant voice in her own headphones. Cherry explained about the needed X-ray.

Captain May's voice said, "Perhaps you'd better come over here—the transmitter . . . No, on second thought, you had definitely better *not* come!" There was a pause, and Cherry heard confused voices over her wire. Then Captain May's voice returned. "All right, Lieutenant Ames. We'll take care of your message."

Cherry hung up. What was happening on Island 13 and at the secret air base, anyway? She tried not to wonder, driving back to her own part of the island.

But thoughts of these two strategic spots were still whirling about in her head when she went to bed that night.

Long after the other girls in the Ritz Stables were asleep, and the blacked-out island was quiet, Cherry tossed restlessly on her cot. At last she fell into a fitful doze, only to waken with a start. She thought—she dreamed—she heard planes! Not guns—she was used to that—but planes!

She staggered out of bed and tiptoed to the door. She had not dreamed that dull hum, it was real! Closer and closer the high-up drone sounded. Enemy planes? Our own? No warning siren roused the island: our own. A swarm of tiny black planes passed distinctly across the face of the moon. One by one, they plunged again into darkness, roared over the island, and were swallowed up in huge night clouds.

Cherry stared until her eyes ached, listened until her ears echoed. But there remained only the man in the moon, winking down at her.

CHAPTER V

A Plane Arrives

THE FIRST OF MARCH WAS A BURNING, GLARING DAY.
Cherry was at work that morning in the Medical Headquarters tent. She was thinking nothing more urgent than that a raw, cold March wind would be welcome here in the tropics. She was completely surprised when, without warning, Major Pierce said to her from the next desk:

"Lieutenant Ames, I nearly forgot to tell you. The Flight Surgeon arrived a couple of days ago at the air base on this island. I met him, and I think you ought to go over and meet him. Now, if it's convenient. Tell him we're sending him the insect spray by jeep. And find out while you're there if there's anything else he wants."

Cherry was delighted. A chance to see the new air base! She jumped up at once to go.

76

Major Pierce grinned at her excitement. "Take my jeep. Get someone to take your place for an hour or so. And give the Flight Surgeon my respects. Verify the spray order, will you?"

"Yes, sir!"

Cherry ran to the supply tent and checked that the spray was being sent. She hailed a passing corpsman and scribbled Ann a note, asking her to take over and listing the duties. Ann's ward did not have many patients this week; the nurse assigned with Ann could handle the ward alone.

Then Cherry jumped into Major Pierce's jeep, and the corpsman driver started off at top speed. She remembered, as the jeep drove northwards, aiming for the tip of the island, that on the day of their arrival Captain May had described the base as only a bare beach. Her black curls whipped against her brilliant red cheeks, her khaki coveralls flapped, and Cherry's curiosity about the base mounted.

They bounced to a stop at the air base, and Cherry clambered out of the jeep, wondering where to find the Flight Surgeon. There were no planes in the sky. But she walked along the beach in amazement.

Here on a wild jungle beach, partly disguised with camouflage nets and movable palm trees, there had sprung up a solid asphalt runway, a strip wide and long enough for the biggest four-engined ships to land on.

There were, half-hidden, huge gasoline drums for refueling; a barracks and mess for the crews and the ground maintenance men; repair shops. Here was a miracle in a month. The Seabees and Engineers had departed long since, so Cherry knew that the Army Air Forces men themselves had built this complete base. In view of all this preparation, it certainly looked as if a big military drive from here was being planned. AAF young men were everywhere, but Cherry headed for the hut with the medical Red Cross painted on its roof.

The Flight Surgeon turned out to be a delightful man, crisp and humorous in manner. Cherry delivered Major Pierce's message, and in a few minutes her business here was completed. Her driver was waiting in the jeep, but Cherry could not resist having a look around before she drove back again. Her lively black eyes fell on some signalmen. She knew one of them slightly, and wandered over to their three-walled hut.

The three signalmen, wearing their heavy helmets for protection against the tropical sun, crouched over the same kind of telephone switchboard Cherry had seen at the Infantry installation. They also worked with a small, heavy, many-dialed instrument which she supposed was a radio for communicating with planes.

"Good morning, Lieutenant West," she said.

"Hello, Lieutenant Ames. Want to see something interesting? Stick around about five minutes and see a Flying Freighter come in!"

"What kind of plane is that?" Cherry inquired.

One of the other young men looked up from the intricate instrument panel and grinned. "A converted, civilian DC–3, only we call it a C–47 in the Army. A transport, one of those big babies that looks as long as a battleship." Cherry's black eyes widened. "Hey, what's that?" the soldier hastily adjusted his headphones and listened. He scowled, and nudged the man next to him. "Bill, I can't make this out. See if you can."

Bill listened, too, but shook his head. Very clearly and deliberately, he spoke landing instructions into a small microphone. Then a tiny hum sounded in their ears, grew louder . They looked up and out over the blue sea, straining their eyes. A speck came into view, disappeared momentarily, then emerged larger and lower than before, and presently became distinguishable as a great, graceful flying ship.

Suddenly a ball of fire dropped from the ship, was swept sideways by the wind, blazed downwards to the water, and was extinguished. The three men beside Cherry shouted, and one seized her elbow.

"A flare! That's a signal there's a wounded man aboard!"

Bill snatched up the field telephone. "Flight Surgeon! Wounded man coming in, sir! We need a stretcher!"

He switched connections, meanwhile asking Cherry rapidly, "Can you medics send us an ambulance? We haven't much equipment, didn't want to duplicate yours——"

At Cherry's nod, he handed the headphones to her. She found herself talking to Major Pierce, asking for an ambulance at once. He asked no questions, but promised that one would be sent immediately.

Bill took the headphones from Cherry. "G–2, G–2," he signaled. "Intelligence Officer, please . . . Hello, this is the air base. You'd better come over here as fast you can, sir. You'll want to make an interrogation."

The huge brown ship was roaring nearer and nearer. Now they could see its twin propellers lazily spinning, the skimming shadow the plane cast upon the water, the fliers' tiny heads silhouetted against sunny plane windows and blue sky.

"Do you think the man is badly wounded? What happened?" Cherry asked.

One of the young men shook his head. "Don't know what happened, but a supply plane is unarmed, you know."

Bill said absently, "Flight Surgeon will have the first look at him," and ran off toward a hut. Cherry, with her professional nurse's readiness to serve, hoped she would be allowed to help, and kept her eyes on the transport.

Now the plane swooped down straight at them, barely clearing the treetops, roaring and throbbing for a moment over their heads. Cherry saw its lowered wheels. It flew lower and lower over the broad runway. Its wheels lightly, unerringly, touched the asphalt, as the pilot carefully set the plane down. The two men beside Cherry sighed with relief. The ship skimmed along the strip, gradually slowed, turned, and slowly taxied back to a white circle painted on the strip, then stopped, its nose facing them. Everyone on the field ran toward the plane.

Running, Cherry happened to glance up into the cabin. Her heart gave a wild leap and she stopped in her tracks. For a moment she could not see, as tears stung her eyes. There, smiling out of a window amidships, was her brother Charlie! Oh, it was too good to be true! Out of the several young men moving inside the plane, dressed identically in sheepskin-lined leather windbreakers and khaki trousers and the jaunty soft-visored cap, Cherry picked out her twin brother! She swelled up so with happiness that she thought she would burst! Charlie saw her; he touched his cap and looked at his sister with grave, glowing blue eyes. Cherry tried to rush forward to him, to the ladder the ground crewmen were lugging to the wide plane door. But she was pushed aside in the commotion.

Men were bringing a stretcher and a first-aid kit, and close on their heels came the Flight Surgeon. Other men followed with coffee and cups and a can of purified water. Ground crew boys in grease-smudged coveralls and ball player's caps were already swarming around the plane and climbing up on the great wings, squinting as they explored the fuselage for bullet or shell holes. Charlie had disappeared back into the cabin again with the stretcher-bearers. Cherry anxiously pushed forward a second time, when someone took a firm grip on her elbow. It was the Intelligence Officer, looking at her with piercing eyes.

"What are you doing here?" he demanded.

Cherry explained. Captain May said, "All right, but you had better wait over here until the ambulance arrives.

Now the first members of the crew were climbing down, Charlie among them, and they were lifting the stretcher gently out of the plane. The wounded soldier struggled, reared back his head, then lay still again. The crewmen watched him, deep concern on their faces, saying under their breaths, "Watch his head." "All right, now?" They lifted him tenderly to the ground. The wounded man blinked in the glaring sunshine and weakly threw one arm across his eyes. Someone who had picked up his cap put it, with a gesture of respect, on the foot of the stretcher. Charlie was looking down at the wounded man, his face working with emotion.

Cherry, forgetting Captain May's admonition, again tried to go forward, eager to help the injured flier, anxious to see her brother. But the Intelligence Officer put a firm hand on her shoulder. "Stand back, Lieutenant, you can't talk to anyone yet," he said tersely. Cherry did not understand.

Now a woman in an Army nurse's uniform was being helped down out of the plane. Cherry realized she must be the unit's new anaesthetist. This woman, too, was prevented from talking to any of the other island people.

An ambulance clanged up on the beach, crunching and rocking along on the sand, and ground to a stop near the plane. Cherry ran over to it. She spoke to the corpsman who was driving and to Captain Willard who had come along.

"I don't know what the man's condition is, Captain Willard," Cherry said, in response to the doctor's question. "He is weak but conscious, he still has a little muscular control, he did not talk—that's all I could observe," she reported.

Captain Willard nodded his gray head and clambered down. "I'll have a look. See, Jack," he explained to the young corpsman who followed him, "the Intelligence Officer is going to hold an interrogation. G–2 tries to find out exactly what happened, while it's still fresh in the fliers' minds. In that way, Intelligence gets a line on what the enemy is doing." He added to Cherry, "You'd better come along with us, Lieutenant Ames."

They knelt beside the patient. As Cherry knelt, her brother patted her head.

"Hello, Sis," he said, his smile very broad and warm.

"Hello, sweetie," Cherry smiled up, pressing his hand. "Be with you in a minute." Then she turned to the patient. Both Captain Willard and the Flight Surgeon were bent over the flier.

Charlie squatted on his heels beside her. "Cherry, isn't there something funny here? Look, he's conscious but he won't talk. Or can't he talk?"

Cherry watched Captain Willard quickly examine the man, especially his head. She saw no mouth wound, no overt sign of a brain wound. Only his shoulder was bleeding a little where a first-aid bandage covered it. The man was exhausted but his eyes were alert and responsive.

"I should think," Cherry answered Charlie slowly, "that he *can* talk. He—he seems sicker than you would expect from that shoulder."

Charlie frowned. "It's strange that he won't talk to any of us."

Suddenly Cherry felt the wounded man's dark blue eyes staring at her. She turned, and from his expression, she knew that he had heard and understood perfectly everything they were saying. There was almost a look of reproach in those eyes. Cherry felt a pang. What was wrong with him?

"All right," said Captain Willard, standing up. "We'll put him in the ambulance right away. Jack——"

The corpsman bent for the stretcher. Charlie sprang to help him, and two other crewmen took the other two handles. Cherry saw that her brother, and the whole crew, was deeply devoted to the wounded man.

"Captain Willard," Cherry asked anxiously, "what's wrong?"

The doctor's honest gray eyes looked back at her. "It's hard to tell, until we have made a complete examination. For now, I'd say the man is exhausted—at the end of his rope both physically and emotionally. I'm surprised that he isn't in shock, he may be within a few minutes. I think that for a while he should have plenty of rest and good food, to build him up. Right now he's in no condition for an operation, if we should find that we have to operate."

"I see," said Cherry. "What can I do, sir?"

The doctor smiled at her. "We'll just put him to bed for a while. So if you want to stay here to see your brother, Lieutenant Ames, you needn't feel you must rush right back with the ambulance."

"Thank you, sir," Cherry said gratefully. "I do want to see my brother. By the way, there's a private room just off Ward M–2, which I fixed up last month for a patient who's discharged now. It's quiet, we could put this flier in there, sir." Captain Willard nodded and turned to go.

Cherry suddenly remembered the new nurse, who was standing around looking rather lost and extremely hot. "And will you take the new nurse back with you, Captain Willard?"

She hurried over to the nurse, who was fanning herself vigorously. "Please forgive me for not meeting you at once," Cherry smiled. "You're the new nurse-anaesthetist for Spencer unit's evacuation hospital, aren't you? I'm Lieutenant Cherry Ames."

The new nurse, although her snug uniform stuck to her and her face was bright red in this tropic heat, returned Cherry's smile with a wide grin. She was a tall, heavily built woman. She had a likable face, fine fair skin, very blue eyes. Her brown hair stuck to her neck in damp ringlets.

"Yes, I'm the anaesthetist," she replied pleasantly. "I'm Mrs. Bessie Flanders, from Albany. Great day! we surely had a time getting here! I never flew before. Guess they thought I'd sink the ship." A gleam of humor lighted up her face as she made mention of her rather vast size. "Well, we got here! Tell me, Lieutenant, who's the Chief Nurse out here?"

"I am," said Cherry. "And I certainly am glad you came. We need you, Lieutenant Flanders. I'll try to make you at home in our rather rough Nurses' Quarters."

"How do, boss," Mrs. Flanders laughed. "Well, I'm all ready to take orders and get to work. Only one thing that bothers me. I hope you won't try to put me on one of those little bitty cots. Those cots just weren't built for Bessie Flanders!"

"Well—" Cherry saw what Bessie meant. "We'll all do our best to make you comfortable. Now if you're ready, the ambulance is starting and it will take you to the hospital grounds. Lieutenant Ann Evans will help you get settled in Nurses' Quarters."

As she helped Mrs. Bessie Flanders into the ambulance, Cherry had a hilarious picture of her crowding into, and probably crowding everyone else out of, the already jammed quarters. She wished that she could be at the Ritz Stables to see the astonished looks on the girls' faces when this veritable Amazon moved in on them. "But right now the real fun—the *important* fun—is that brother of mine."

Cherry hoped that now, at last, she could turn to Charlie. But the Intelligence Officer was herding the men from the plane into a tight little knot, and waving everyone else away. Cherry went up the beach with several AAF men, and drifted away from them. She looked back at the group around the plane.

The Intelligence Officer was talking earnestly, searching their faces, and everyone from the plane was staring at him in the deepest concentration. The airmen were talking too, consulting one another, visibly making efforts to think, to remember. Charlie held up both arms and described an arc, then a plunge. Captain May was taking notes.

Finally the interrogation was over. Charlie promptly made a dash for his sister. Cherry ran too. They met in a joyous bear hug.

Cherry stepped back and took a good, long, satisfying look at her twin brother. Charlie had the same pert, lively face as Cherry's, in a firmer masculine version. His eyes were intensely blue, with the keen gaze of focusing on far distances. His short, rumpled hair was fair, and burned even lighter by the sun. He was tall and broad-shouldered, thinner than when Cherry had last seen him, at home, in September. Secretly she thought that his young face looked a little worn. But he had his old, easy, breezy manner, with the seriousness hidden underneath.

"You're as brown as an Indian!" he laughed at her. "But too thin."

"You're too thin yourself," she retorted. "Seen the parents since I did?"

"No, but they're all right. Here's a letter from Mother that you can read later."

"Where've you been?" Cherry demanded, stuffing the letter in the pocket of her coveralls.

"You're as bad as the Intelligence Officer! Well, I've been mostly on the banana route, from Panama. Just missed you there, pal. This trip is a five-day supply route, but we go in relays and rest at each stop. We started from outside Miami, went to South America, dropped supplies in India, dropped supplies in China, and finally drop supplies here. So if I look tired after *this* trip," Charlie grinned shrewdly, "don't scold me, Nurse. I'll rest up."

Cherry linked her arm through his, and the Ames twins hung on to each other, beaming.

"You old lug," Cherry said affectionately.

"The same to you! Brought you a lovely new portable X-ray for a present. Also some strychnine and quinine, Say, do you know what else we were ferrying when we were shot at today? Gasoline and ammunition. We'd have gone up like confetti if the Japs' aim had been better."

Cherry looked at the huge supply transport, being unloaded now, and shivered. She looked back thankfully at her brother, and suddenly noticed the new silver bar on his shoulder.

"Why, congratulations! I certainly am slow! You're a first lieutenant now—we both are!"

Charlie explained. "You see, when I was a gunner, I was staff sergeant, still an enlisted man. Then I was a gunnery officer, and a second lieutenant. Now they transferred me to the ATC and I'm not a gunner for now——"

"But isn't that an awful waste, to train a gunner and then not let him, uh, gun? I mean, shoot?"

"Honey, when the Army needs men for a particular job in a hurry," Charlie told her, "they have to take the first men they can find. Right now, I'm more needed in supply work than as a gunner. The wounded flier, Lieutenant Grant, is trained both as a gunner and as a pilot, but he's needed more urgently to supervise the shipping of guns. Even more than he's needed in combat just now. See? Come on over and meet the crew."

As they walked over to the young men around the plane, Cherry said happily, "It certainly is a coincidence that you landed on my island."

"Coincidence, nothing!" Charlie said coolly. "I figured out from your APO address and from what other fliers knew that you must be on Island 14. So when I got a chance at this assignment, I jumped at it. Gentlemen, this is my sister, Lieutenant Cherry Ames, Chief Nurse—" Charlie could hardly keep the pride out of his voice. "Captain Keller, Lieutenant Brown, Lieutenant McCarthy——"

Cherry shook hands with her brother's crew and smiled into six friendly, intelligent young faces. She noticed that they all had the same keen look about the eyes. Fliers' eyes.

"Tell us, Lieutenant Cherry," said Captain Keller, the pilot and commander of the plane. "Will Gene— Lieutenant Grant—be all right? The wounded man? He's an awfully valuable man. He's a specialist in charge of gun cargo and he's copilot of our transport."

Cherry saw the anxiety in their faces. She replied, "No one can guarantee that. But I promise I'll do everything in my power for him."

They all had to move aside, for the ground crew were hitching the plane to a truck and were slowly dragging the great transport, still half-loaded, off to the woods. Cherry guessed there must be a concealed hangar, where repairs and overhauling could be done. She was wondering how long Charlie and his crew would be here, feeling reluctant to ask, when Charlie asked the same thing aloud.

"Our cannonball will be in and out of here several times in the next few weeks," the pilot said. "We're going to be ferrying a lot of gasoline, ammunition, and machinery in here. But mum's the word!"

Cherry grinned happily at her brother. They'd be seeing each other a few times! The pilot added that they probably would be gone again, immediately, for a few days, and their appearances and reappearances here would be extremely irregular. Cherry did not mind—

Charlie would be here! She was so happy that she failed to realize, for the moment, what all that extra gasoline and ammunition would be used for and the reasons for the secrecy.

It was only on her way back to the hospital that she began to think—about this, and about what the injured flier's strangely exhausted condition might mean. If it was mystery she wanted, here it was.

CHAPTER VI

~~~~~~

Bessie

RIGHT OFF, THE GIRLS ALL LIKED BESSIE. THEY COULD not help liking someone who was always laughing and poking fun at herself, even though Bessie Flanders' generous size undoubtedly crowded the Ritz Stables.

"You should have provided a skyscraper for me," Bessie said the evening she had moved in. "I'm nearly six feet tall and proportioned to match. I'll dust the rafters for you, with ease. No extra charge, either! Yes, sir, there's plenty of Bessie!"

"Never mind," Cherry said, helping her unpack her footlocker. "I think we're going to like every inch of you."

"And every pound," Bessie reminded her, laughing. "Say, girls, I'll bet I weigh more than any two of you put together."

"Bet you don't," said plump Bertha Larsen, but she looked hopeful.

"Bet I do," said Bessie. "Look at this!" Gingerly she eased herself down on the cot assigned to her. The cot squeaked loudly in protest, sagged, swayed, and one wooden leg slipped. "See?" Bessie demanded. Her face twinkled with humor, and she brushed her soft brown hair off her damp neck. Cherry bent to help her fix the cot leg. "Now what are you girls going to do with all this woman? That is, if I don't melt away in all this heat first."

The girls looked at her uncertainly, unwilling to join her jokes about herself for fear of hurting her feelings.

"Oh, don't be so polite," Bessie teased them, as she struggled out of her too-tight slacks. "I know I am—er—monumental!"

"We-ell," Ann said carefully, "because of your size, you may suffer more than the rest of us from the heat here."

"We won't feed her," Gwen said promptly, with her careless humor. "Then she'll be thin—and comfortable."

Bessie wailed. "I just love to eat!"

"Certainly you do," Cherry said a little sharply. "I want you to eat properly, and keep well and strong."

Bessie flexed a bicep in her smooth white arm. "I'm strong, see? I don't need to eat. I'll diet and become thin and graceful as a string bean."

"No dieting. You eat! That's an order," the Chief Nurse told her. "And here's another order. Please come over to Headquarters tent first thing tomorrow morning, and we'll go over your records and get you assigned to duty."

The next morning, Cherry learned several interesting things about her new nurse-anaesthetist, as she interviewed her. As Chief Nurse, Cherry had to find out what this nurse's training and experience had been and what branches of nursing work she could do. For the anaesthetist work in Operating hut probably would not fill all of Lieutenant Flanders' eight daily working hours. A well-trained nurse should be able to treat any sort of medical case.

"Sit down, won't you?" Cherry said pleasantly to Mrs. Flanders in the Medical Headquarters tent that morning. She added hastily, "Not on that box—I think you'd be more comfortable on this folding chair."

"You mean the box won't hold me," Bessie laughed at herself. "Do you know what happened this morning? I sat down on little Mai Lee's bench, in Nurses' Quarters, and now there's nothing left of it but splinters!"

Cherry could not help laughing.

"And the splinters are mostly in me!" Bessie added. "Now, boss, what do you want to know about me— besides what I weigh? The girls are already calling me

Skinny!" She fanned herself as she talked, her pleasant face flushed and perspiring.

"I want to know practically everything about you." Cherry smiled back at the woman's good humor. She took Mrs. Flanders' records out of her file. "Where did you have your training?"

The new nurse told her that she had trained, about ten years ago, at Birdwing, a small hospital. Then she had married, and except for helping the Red Cross in emergencies, she had done no nursing since. A year ago, her husband was killed in action. Bessie's first thought had been to return to nursing. She had wasted no time on grief, she only wanted to serve. Since she had no children, she was free to nurse anywhere. At first it was hard, for she had to take refresher courses and to learn new techniques which had been discovered in the years of her retirement from the profession. Bessie, for all her joking, was very serious and realized that medical and nursing science had improved, in some branches had changed completely, since she had trained.

"So I went back into a civilian hospital at first," Mrs. Flanders told Cherry. "They certainly do need more nurses! My, there are lots of older, retired, patriotic nurses returning to help out in this shortage. Some of them grandmothers, that's how shorthanded we are. The real young student nurses are a great help. Well, then I thought I'd like to get into the Army Nurse Corps.

So I applied, and they nearly marched the feet off me, and taught me how to crawl on my tummy under fire and—and, well, here I am."

"Here you are, and we certainly are glad to have you," Cherry said. "We need you for everything from doing dressings to assisting at neurosurgery."

Bessie rolled up her sleeves and pushed back the curling tendrils of brown hair. "Just tell me where to start," she said, her eyes very blue and eager. "You know, it's a new experience for me, having a boss as young as you are. I'll bet you youngsters look on me as an old fossil. Well, let me tell you, ma'am, I'm not as young as the rest of you but there's plenty of work left in old Flanders yet!"

Cherry leaned toward her across the rough desk, genuinely pleased. "I'm glad you feel that way! We need nurses terribly, you'll see for yourself. And I—I personally am glad to have a mature nurse here. There's many a time I could use an older and wiser head than mine."

For a moment, a motherly look softened Bessie's pretty, round face. "I don't know how wise my head is, but I—I'm not just a clown, for all my fooling and my—my size."

Cherry stood up to indicate that the interview was at an end. "I do wish you'd stop making fun of yourself," she said gently. "Let's see, I'll have your schedule for you by late this afternoon. In the meantime, would you please go to the Operating hut and make supplies and drains? And if any of the ward nurses ask, you might give them a hand till you have your own ward."

Bessie stooped to duck under the tent doorway. "Yes, boss. And if you hear any laughing from the ward, you'll know who's in there!" She went out, knocking over a pile of supplies on her way. She turned around to Cherry, making a face. "You see?" she called back. "Dainty as an elephant—that's Bessie!" And she patiently picked everything up.

Cherry did indeed hear laughter from some of the wards and from Operating hut. She could hear Bessie's booming, hearty voice, too. Bessie, or "Skinny" as everyone was promptly calling her, must be at her nonsense of joking about her size. Whatever it was, the laughter was a good thing.

Later that day, Marie Swift, who was still weak from her recent illness, came to Cherry and said, "That new nurse is a darling! Do you know that she did almost all my ward work for me this morning? And how the patients enjoyed having her around! Bessie Flanders is worth her weight in gold—even all *that* weight!"

Cherry learned, too, that Bessie was quick and handy in Operating hut, getting things ready for operations. "She's so big," one of the nurses said, "you'd think she'd be slow. She did knock a few things over, but she's surprisingly fast and light on her feet—for such a big woman."

Major Pierce, too, found the new nurse a real asset to the unit.

Everyone, within a few days, was calling the good-humored and pretty Bessie "Skinny." It puzzled Cherry a little, for Bessie was not really fat. She was, rather, a tall, big-boned woman, well-covered with solid flesh, and not fat at all. In fact, Cherry thought, Bessie was a majestic Amazon of a woman, who might have been queenly if she had stood up straight and proud. Instead, Bessie stooped, as if ashamed of her size, when she should have walked like a goddess. This stooping did make her appear awkward, and besides, she constantly made derogatory remarks about her appearance. The others naturally took her at her word. Bessie said that she was fat and funny-looking, and she said it so often, and she believed it so firmly herself, that everyone else believed it too. Except Cherry, who secretly thought Bessie handsome.

But within the next week, even Cherry had to laugh. Bessie really did have comical troubles. Every night, regularly as lights out, her cot collapsed. There would be creaks and groans in the dark in the Ritz Stables, half-humorous, half-disgusted mutterings from Bessie, and then, sooner or later, the inevitable crash. On would go the lights, the girls would spring up from their cots, and there, grinning up at everybody from the floor, would be Bessie in a tangle of sheets and mosquito netting.

"Well, that was a short night's sleep," Bessie would say, unwinding herself from the debris and scrambling to her feet and her full height. "I'll take a lower berth, conductor. And a larger. Ah, well, I'm getting used to this."

It was true that Bessie's cot had collapsed under her on Monday, Tuesday, Wednesday and Thursday. The girls had been sympathetic at first but by now, even the Chief Nurse had to admit, Bessie's predicament was just plain funny. The girls put two cots together and after that, Bessie slept on those. The two cots survived her but Bessie announced that the crack where they joined, in spite of the thick padding over it, was leaving a permanent ridge down her spine.

"Remember the princess and the pea in the fairy tale?" Bessie joked, "That's me, just a delicate little thing!"

Bessie stumbled and fell in the stream. The girls fished her out and peeled her wet, tight uniform off her. Then they found that all her other clothes were in the laundry, and none of theirs were big enough to fit her. Bessie spent the rest of that afternoon in a uniform borrowed from one of the infantrymen. It was the oddest fit ever seen on Island 14.

"I look like a comic valentine!" Bessie declared, giggling. "My patients are going to get a good laugh out of this!" They did, too, and Bessie did not seem to mind. But Bessie did not show up at Mess for supper that night, Cherry noticed.

That night, for all her enjoyment of Bessie's antics, Cherry had more serious matters on her mind. This was the evening when she had "made time" to spend with the wounded airman.

Cherry had been to see him briefly, several times each day, with Captain Willard. The doctor had said, "Exhaustion—flier's nerve strain," and prescribed sedatives so that the tense man could fall asleep. Cherry saw to it that he had plenty of milk and good food when he awoke. She assigned Ann, who was calm and cheerful, and a dependable corpsman, to look after this patient.

When Cherry tiptoed into the flier's quiet isolation tent that hot evening, she whispered to Ann, "How is he?"

Ann shook her head. "He won't talk. I wish he would talk! I try to encourage him to get things off his chest, but he hasn't said a syllable. It seems hopeless." She turned over the chart to Cherry and prepared to leave.

Hopeless. That was the word Mrs. Flanders had used, too, when Cherry asked her what she thought of the patient's condition. Neither Ann nor Bessie Flanders were persons to use that word without thought.

After Ann had left, Cherry sat down by the flier's bedside and studied him. He had a finely modeled face, smooth satiny brown hair and brows, a nervous, sensitive mouth. He was in his early twenties. Even with his eyes closed. Cherry saw in his face uncommon intelligence and feeling and dignity. His shoulder was heavily bandaged. X-rays showed that the shoulder would require an operation. Cherry was delicately examining the bandage when she had the curious feeling that he was staring at her. She turned slightly. His dark blue eyes, heavy with fatigue, were open now and looking at her.

"Hello," Cherry said, mustering up a poise she did not feel. "Are you feeling better? You look better," she said untruthfully.

His gaze did not flicker. Had he understood her?

"Gene," Cherry said gently. "You know Charlie Ames in your crew. I'm Charlie's sister, Cherry."

Still there was no reply, no sign of response, though those heavy-lidded eyes registered perfect comprehension. There was a terrible silence in the tent. The footsteps outside seemed to come from another world.

"Gene," Cherry insisted, fighting down her own fear "It's me, Charlie's sister. It's Cherry. Don't be afraid."

But it was not fear in those eyes that followed the slightest bend of her head, the smallest quiver of expression on her rosy face. It might have been memory, lost and dim, which dropped a screen of silence between the flier and Cherry. He did not speak, he did not move, only followed her with those haunted eyes. He was so tired it was work for him to breathe. Cherry gave him a sedative. Presently he slept.

Hopeless, Mrs. Flanders had said, and Ann had said. But she refused to accept "hopeless" as the verdict. She had promised his crew to get him well! Perhaps he would be better after more rest and after an operation on his shoulder. Perhaps then he would talk. Cherry began to look forward to the day the flier would be strong enough to endure surgery.

Meanwhile there were other operations. Cherry began to spend more and more of her time in the Operating hut, working as O.R. supervisor with the new anaesthetist, and the surgeons and assisting doctors and other operating nurses who were scheduled on any particular day. Bessie Flanders turned out to be an excellent anaesthetist, cooperative, almost intuitive, in working with the doctor. Over a period of time, wounded soldiers were brought in from the fighting forward islands. The most amazing surgeries were performed.

The most common surgeries were the removal of shrapnel fragments from exploding shells. But there were also a perforated ulcer, a delicate skin graft, fractured

arms and legs, an arm with lacerated nerves which had
to be tied together again. There was even, in this jungle
hut, one infected brain wound, where the team of
doctors and nurses held their breaths while Major
Pierce cleansed the wound, grafted leg tissues over the
skull gap, and saved the patient from paralysis and
blindness. No finer neurosurgery could have been done
in the most modern hospital at home.

Cherry found her work an inspiration. But there was
still one discouraging factor. The Commanding Officer
still continued his daily, seemingly unnecessary rounds
of the evacuation hospital. For the past few days he had
been concentrating his fretful comments on Major
Pierce. The harassed unit director hinted several times
that Colonel Pillsbee's endless inspections wasted a
great deal of precious time. But there was no getting rid
of his stalking, birdlike figure.

After one particularly trying session with Colonel
Pillsbee, Bessie announced flatly, "*I* think he ought to
leave it to Major Pierce to inspect!"

"Hmm," said Cherry, and Major Pierce said, "Very
interesting," and strolled resignedly away.

And then, rather abruptly, Bessie changed. The older
nurse seemed to lose some of her high good humor
and to change her mind about Colonel Pillsbee, too.
The climax came one night in the Ritz Stables, when
Mrs. Flanders delivered quite a lecture to the girls.

It came out of a blue sky, and the girls all were amazed to hear her say, crossly:

"Oh, stop grumbling about Colonel Pillsbee! He's a fine man and you should value him at his true worth. You youngsters have no right to be calling him The Pill, and such things. He——"

"Pill is just a medical term," Gwen assured her with a straight face.

"He's a good, kind, responsible man," Bessie scolded, as they listened in astonishment. "You're all too young to understand his viewpoint."

"Maybe so," Gwen conceded, "but couldn't we talk about something else now? Or—I'll tell you what—let's sing! *Wa-ay down u-pon the Swa-NEE Ri-ver——*"

Several not very melodious voices warbled along with Gwen's. Bessie beat her hands together for silence.

"If you *can't* sing, *don't* sing!" she said sourly. The girls stared. Good-humored Bessie—cranky!

"Whatever came over her?" Vivian whispered to Cherry.

"Never saw her like this before," Ann murmured. "Something must be wrong."

They watched Bessie paddle around the stable in her bare feet and old-fashioned cambric nightgown. She stumbled over big Bertha, who was washing her stockings in her helmet. She grunted as if Bertha had no right to be where *she* chose to stumble. "Besides, I should think nurses would have more consideration! Good night!"

In the darkness of the Ritz Stables, Cherry felt several hands nudge her and she was hastily escorted outside for a whispered conference.

"Boss, we'd better tell you. We've been working in the wards next to Bessie's and we know what's the matter with her."

"She's been cross like this for some time, only you haven't been with her to see it."

"Look here, Cherry, you *must* do something! We've tried and failed. Now, you're the boss—you *insist!*"

"Cherry Ames, you must do something about poor Bessie immediately."

Cherry whispered back frantically, "Do what, for goodness sake? What's wrong?"

"Bessie is dieting—she's not eating anything to speak of," the girls told the Chief Nurse. "Bessie is cranky because she's hungry!"

"So that's it!" Cherry sighed with relief. "If that's all, we'll just feed her. You had me worried there! I thought Bessie was planning mutiny, or something."

But it was not so simple to persuade Bessie to eat. The girls tried, in a group; Ann and Bertha tried, individually; Cherry tried. But Bessie persisted in staying away from Mess. The girls brought her trays of food, from Mess to the Ritz Stables. Bessie refused everything, except black coffee and green vegetables, which were not enough nourishment.

"From hippopotamus to sylph, by the easy road of starvation," Bessie insisted, with a gleam of her old humor.

"You'll be neither a hippo nor a sylph if you don't eat," Cherry warned her. "You'll be sick."

"Pooh! Me, sick? I'm as strong as a horse—but I'm tired of looking like a horse. No, boss. No, fellow nurses. Bessie diets!"

"I'll tell Major Pierce on you!" Cherry threatened.

"Why, the Major himself teased me about being so big," Bessie retorted. But her usual merry smile was missing. And now Cherry understood.

Bessie might joke about her size but she was sensitive about it all the same. Cherry wanted to talk to her sensibly about her wrong ideas of her appearance. But to do so in front of the assembled nurses would be tactless. She would have to do it the next day.

When the next day came, Cherry remembered excitedly that this was the day the wounded flier was to be brought in for an operation.

Cherry herself had scheduled this operation, at Captain Willard's request. She assigned two of the gentlest corpsmen to carry the still-silent flier from his bed to Surgical, on a field stretcher mounted on bicycle wheels. Cherry herself was going to administer the anaesthetic.

In the little draped-off section that was the ether room, Cherry stood talking quietly to the silent airman. His eyes, fastened on her face, slowly closed as the preliminary morphine relaxed him. Cherry kept her hand on his pulse, from time to time lifting the flap to peer into the bigger room.

The Operating hut was in readiness. The inner wall, and even the outer wall, had been scrubbed. The high operating table under its powerful center lamps was draped with sterile sheets and blankets. A sterile (or germ-free) nurse, her face and hair masked with gauze, sterile rubber gloves on her hands, lifted from the sterilizers gauzes and sutures for the surgeon's use. There were heaps of white gauze, white swabs, white sheeting, bandages, towels. Marie Swift came in quietly, also masked. Cherry had asked her to be operating nurse, for Marie was excellent, and Cherry, who wanted to be with the flier when he lost consciousness under ether, would not have time to scrub up to be operating nurse herself. A corpsman, and Bessie Flanders, masked too but in non-sterile garb, worked around the end of the hut as circulating nurse, adjusting lights and faucets and spraying antiseptic on the canvas-covered dirt floor. The air in here was hot and sweetish, smelling of soap and chemicals and ether. Cherry glanced down watchfully at the patient. The flier was almost asleep, breathing deeply, holding fast to her hand.

She heard Major Pierce and Captain Willard scrubbing up at the sinks. The other operating tables in the hut were unmade, their lights darkened. The surgeons were concentrating on this one operation. Cherry wondered why. The X-rays had shown shrapnel fragments embedded in his shoulder. Probing for these would be a painful and serious enough operation but not crucial. Did the surgeons expect to find something else wrong? Cherry glanced down at Gene's sensitive, drawn face and felt a wave of pity.

It was almost time. The corpsman pulled a triple flap over the entrance and dropped a heavy mosquito bar over that. The air in here became stiflingly hot.

Now Major Pierce and Captain Willard came in, careful not to touch anything. While Marie slipped on their squeaking rubber gloves and sterile coats for them, and tightened their masks, Cherry and the corpsman wheeled in the sleeping flier. They half-lifted, half-rolled him onto the operating table. Three powerful lights shone down brilliantly on his face. The rest of the hut was darkened. Everyone but the two surgeons stepped back into the shadows. Marie stood close behind Major Pierce with the needed supplies. There was a hush of expectancy. Major Pierce nodded to Cherry.

Cherry, standing ready at the patient's head, with the wheeled, balloonlike gas-oxygen machine, began to administer the anaesthetic. Presently she said, "The patient is under, sir."

"Pulse?" Major Pierce asked under his breath.

Cherry murmured, "Pulse slow. Respiration shallow. Blood pressure low." It was not an auspicious beginning. She glanced at the gas-oxygen machine's reading, then at the oxygen tank, standing by in case of emergency. Marie was exposing the shoulder, cleaning it and swabbing it with iodine, and making a cradle of sterile sheets around it.

"X-rays," Major Pierce ordered.

Bessie Flanders held the X-rays up to the powerful lights. The two surgeons frowned at them. The X-rays were, as everyone here knew from a previous look at them, puzzlingly unclear.

"Strange," Captain Willard said to Major Pierce. "That flesh wound was never made by ordinary shrapnel balls." He pointed with a scalpel close to the X-ray. "And those are no ordinary fragments that you can see close to the bone, either."

"It's darned funny," Major Pierce muttered. "Well, we'll have a look at the shoulder itself."

Dr. Willard made the incision, a thin white line ran down the fleshy part of the flier's shoulder close to the armpit. Quickly the veins were tied off so that there was no bleeding. The operating nurse handed Major Pierce retractors to hold the incision open while the surgeon worked. The operation had begun. Cherry as anaesthetist constantly kept checking her patient's condition, ready to warn the surgeons of any drastic change.

The two surgeons probed and studied the shoulder. All the others respectfully stood by, silent, alert to assist, watching every move.

"Look at this!" Major Pierce said suddenly, and lifted up his pronged instrument. Between the prongs glistened a tiny, jagged, silvery piece of metal. "I've never seen shrapnel balls that acted like this. Look here, Willard——"

The two men excitedly bent their heads under the fiery bright lights, and as they intently removed the bit of metal, discussed something in rapid, low voices. Cherry could not quite hear them, nor see into the wound, for she of course kept her place in the shadows, a little beyond the patient's head.

Major Pierce straightened up and said clearly, "All right, we'll try that."

The surgeons cleaned out the wound, and after a long time succeeded in removing all the dirt and more particles of metal. They packed the wound with sulfa. Now, Cherry thought, they will sew up the wound. But instead, the surgeons looked again at the surfaces of the shoulder. Pin-prick points were torn in the front of the shoulder, but at the back there was a gaping tear.

Suddenly Cherry remembered something. She said respectfully, "Major Pierce." Both surgeons looked up. No subordinate ever spoke during an operation, except to say something urgent.

"Do you recall," Cherry said hesitantly, "a directive you received from Washington recently? It asked all Army doctors to be on the lookout for strange wounds which might indicate new or strange enemy weapons."

Major Pierce whistled under his breath, and Captain Willard said, "By George, that's so!"

Major Pierce rapidly began to close the wound, speaking softly. "Right you are, there *is* something mysterious here, Lieutenant Ames. Captain Willard and I have a lot of doubts and questions about this case. We can't understand those small holes in front on entering and the large tear at the back." He worked in silence over the patient, then added, "We'll report immediately to Colonel Pillsbee and turn the fragments over to him. Lieutenant Ames, see that these are placed in a container."

"Yes, sir," Cherry replied, keeping her eyes and hand on the flier. She nodded to Bessie who stepped forward and picked up the precious fragments. "The patient's pulse is weak, sir," Cherry informed the surgeon.

Major Pierce ordered adrenalin. Marie gave the hypodermic, and the wound was, with some difficulty, finally closed and dressed. The flier seemed in a fairly satisfactory condition as Dr. Willard and two corpsmen wheeled him back to the isolation tent. Ann was there; she and a corpsman would stay with him.

Only after the surgeons had left, and Cherry had dismissed Marie and the nurse and the corpsman, did she allow herself to think of the mystery here. Mrs. Flanders cleaned up the table, while Cherry sterilized and put away instruments. Bessie was crossly silent, so Cherry had a chance to think about the shattering discovery this might be.

"Not so fast," Cherry warned herself. "We haven't discovered anything yet. There's only a suspicion. But a strange wound, plus strange fragments, plus Gene's uncanny silence—it all begins to add up. It looks as if——"

Bessie softly groaned. Cherry was startled out of her thoughts. She dropped the instruments she was wiping, and ran around to the other side of the hut.

"Bessie! Bessie, what is it?"

The older woman's face was wan and drawn. She was leaning weakly against the wall, her eyes almost closed. Cupped in her hand were two tiny pieces of metal. "Careless of me," she started to say. Cherry, noticing that Bessie was on the verge of fainting, grasped the fragments and shoved them into her pocket. She led Bessie to a chair and made her sit down.

"Are you sick, Bessie?"

"No—not sick——"

"I know what's the matter with you," Cherry said, trying to repress a giggle. "You're hungry."

Bessie weakly nodded. "So hungry I'm faint. Go on, scold me."

"No, I'm not going to scold you. I'm going to feed you. Can you walk over to Mess with me? Here, lean on my arm, you—you dieter!"

Mess Hall was deserted. Cherry sat Bessie down at the long rough table, and wheedled some light, warm food from the cook. She brought it back, and sat beside her nurse while she ate. It was strange to see big Bessie so weak and pale. She confessed that she had eaten scarcely anything substantial for nearly two weeks now.

"I'm sorry I was—irritable," she said as she finished her food. "But—you see—I'm so tired of people poking fun at me because I'm fat."

"No one would have thought of you as fat, if you had not started it yourself," Cherry pointed out. "You were never fat."

"But I *am* fat! I'm huge—awkward—funny-looking—" Bessie could not laugh about it now. Real distress filled her blue eyes.

"You are very attractive and it's about time you realized it," Cherry said firmly.

"Wha-a-at!"

"Yes, you are. Why, Bessie, *every* girl has her own kind of good looks. Wouldn't you agree that a brunette can be as beautiful as a blonde?"

"Ye-es," Bessie agreed cautiously.

"Well, there's no one standard for beauty, you see. There are all kinds of beauty. You happen to be tall and have a large frame to match your height. What's wrong with that? It's magnificent, in its own way."

"But I—but I'm so *big!*"

"Then why don't you make an asset of your liability?" Cherry suggested. "Queens are supposed to be tall, aren't they? Those handsome models whose photographs you see in all the magazines—they're as big and bigger than you. Our swimming stars and tennis stars, whom the whole United States admires, are mostly stunning Amazons of girls. If you'd only accept yourself, Bessie, and cultivate your own particular brand of good looks—Why, my heavens," Cherry said, laughing, "every girl is sure that she, and she alone, has some awful flaw in her appearance. Ten to one, no one else ever noticed or even thought that feature was a flaw at all!"

Bessie thought for a moment. Then she said shyly, "My husband thought I was nice-looking. And—and some of my friends think so."

"There, you see! If you'd stand up straight and be proud of your height, instead of stooping—and if you'd try not to bump into things, or take a little exercise—" Cherry stopped and laughed again. "Sometimes I think good looks is partly a state of mind. Now see, you called attention to your size, so everyone thought of you as fat. When you are not fat at all! If *you* thought of *yourself* as nice-looking, you'd convince other people that you are. And you really, truly are, you know."

Bessie blinked hard, and there was a suspicious moisture in her eyes. "I feel much happier about the whole thing," she admitted.

"And no more dieting," Cherry reminded her with a grin.

"No more dieting," and Bessie added, as she rose with confidence from the mess table to her full, proud height, "because I don't need to diet. I'm *meant* to be big!"

Cherry, walking down the coral-edged road to the Medical Headquarters tent, felt almost as much satisfaction in Bessie's new self-confidence as Bessie herself.

~~~~~~

CHAPTER VII

The Silent Flier

WITHOUT WARNING ONE NIGHT, CHARLIE CAME BACK.

Cherry was working alone, late, in the Medical Headquarters tent. She had been wondering when, if ever, her brother was going to return to Island 14. Suddenly there he was, filling the canvas doorway, his tall active figure, his keen blue eyes, his wind-blown hair, the very picture of air and speed and danger.

"Hi," he said, as casually as if he had seen her yesterday and had not been risking his life in between times.

"Hi," Cherry said faintly, in astonishment. "Well, well, Lieutenant A., where've *you* been?" She jumped up, smiling, trying to hide her relief. She formally offered him a chair, made of a crate, while he took a good tug at her black curls.

117

"Oh, here and there," her brother teased her. He caught her frown as she sat down, and he sighed. "Oh, all right! My team's been flying a lot or stuff—plane parts, heavy trucks, tires, blood plasma—and some more men. Something certainly is up. You all right, Sis?"

"I'm fine. *I* haven't been flying at twenty-five thousand feet, above the Himalayas like you. How are *you?* Don't you freeze up there?"

Charlie smoothed his light hair and grinned. "It's cold, all right. But we have fur-lined flying suits. So I'm okay."

"Any Japs up there in the clouds?" Cherry asked cautiously.

Charlie looked annoyed. Cherry knew he did not like her to worry about him—her doubts filtered doubts into his own courage. "No Japs this trip. We fly awfully high to avoid 'em. You know, we're unarmed, transports always are. Say, tell me—" his face grew very serious— "how's Gene?"

Cherry leaned her rosy cheek on her hand and looked squarely at her brother. "Not good, Charlie," she said. "Not good at all. Oh, I don't mean physically— physically, he's coming along very nicely. But—he—I hate to tell you this about your friend—I think something has hurt his spirit."

Charlie scowled. "You girls and your roundabout way of talking! What in thunder do you mean?"

"I mean," Cherry said earnestly, "he won't talk. He lies there and seems to be brooding about something and never says a word. It—it gives me the creeps."

Charlie looked down at his hands, studied them with exaggerated care. "I can tell you something," he said at last. "Matter of fact, it's something you probably already know, at least in theory, only this is the first time you've run smack up against it. It's this. A man can stand only so much strain, then he gets tired and nervous, and just—wilts, goes to pieces temporarily. It's called combat fatigue, or nerve strain, what they used to call shell shock in World War I, only that's an inaccurate word. And Gene has been flying and fighting too long. He had one of the most dangerous and nerve-racking jobs there are—tail gunner. Those boys are the ones who do the real fighting. It's an awful emotional tension; I know. Gene's been a pilot, too. Well, the Flight Surgeon wanted to ground him for a rest, because a person can take only so much. But Gene wouldn't hear of being grounded. When the rest of us switched to the Air Transport Command, he insisted on coming right along. He was overtired when he started. Gene's had too many harrowing hours in the air without rest. He's exhausted, that's all."

Cherry said slowly, "No, that isn't all." And she told her brother about the strange metal fragments the surgeons had taken from Gene's shoulder, and the strange wound. Charlie's face tightened as she carefully described it. "So that's why I think," she concluded, "that Gene is brooding over something the rest of us know nothing about."

"Strange," Charlie muttered. "It's downright mysterious."

"Mysterious certainly is the word. Now tell me," Cherry demanded briskly, "every single thing you can remember about the flight on which Gene was wounded."

"All right, honey, I'll do my best." Charlie hitched his crude chair closer to Cherry's desk, thought for a moment, then began.

"We were about forty minutes away from Island 14. We were in the general direction of those forward islands, where you hear the guns from, but we circled away as much as we could. Everything seemed to be going all right. Gene went back alone to the middle of the ship to check some cargo that was rattling around. The rest of us were way up front. Then all of a sudden, the plane sort of rocked, for no reason I could see. It could have been a shot, or it could have been an air pocket that rocked us. The noise of the propellers and engines might have drowned out the sound of a shot, you know. Gene said—" Charlie drew his blond brows together "—Gene said, 'There they are, boys! Enemy aircraft!'" He fell silent.

"Go on," Cherry prompted.

"It doesn't make sense. The rest of us took a quick look all around us. There *weren't* any enemy planes. There wasn't any smoke, any fire. *There wasn't anything!*"

"What did he say?"

"Nothing. He never spoke again."

Cherry buried her face in her hands. She tried to think but the flier's drawn face, especially his haunted eyes, kept rising up on her closed eyelids. She opened her eyes hastily to wipe out that pathetic vision.

"Charlie," she said in a choked voice, "there's no sense in our getting upset about this. We've got to keep our wits, if we're going to help him. And the way to help Gene is to find out what happened. Gene saw or experienced something the rest of you didn't see. To cure Gene, we've got to solve this mystery."

Charlie laughed mirthlessly. "Think you can solve it? Let me tell you something, Sis. There's more to this than saving just this one man. If the enemy has a secret weapon, then the lives of thousands of men are at stake!"

Cherry shuddered, then drew herself up. "All right, the first thing is to keep a cool head. The enemy would just love to get us all scared and panicky. But facts *can* be uncovered, and, for Gene's sake if for no other reason, we must get to the bottom of this." She hesitated a moment, then asked, "What's Gene like when he's well?"

"The finest man you ever knew," Charlie replied softly. "Cherry, we fellows all think he's swell. He's so quiet and good and modest and unselfish. I could tell you things he's done for us, at risk to himself—And he never did talk much. Sort of kept his thoughts to himself. But when he did talk, it was highly intelligent talk. Still, no one ever really knew him." Charlie's voice grew rough. "Gene was always sort of—remote. And now he's farther away than ever."

"Hold tight!" Cherry commanded. "We'll get Gene to talk again! We're going to solve this mystery, or my name isn't Ames."

"My name is Ames, too," Charlie reminded her. "Let's go!"

Brother and sister settled down at the desk and soberly went over the facts they had between them. Charlie said the Intelligence Officer was disturbed because the crew could not give him an adequate report of what had happened. Captain May had been questioning them until their heads ached, trying to jog their memories. More interrogations were coming.

Cherry could not report much, only that the wounded flier was merely sleeping and eating, slowly regaining his strength, the shoulder slowly healing. She could have sworn that he knew perfectly well what was said to him, and that his failure to reply was no lack of comprehension, but came from another source. But what source? Shock? Yes, probably hysterical muteness caused by shock. Cherry suggested: either he did not want to talk, lest he would have to talk about what he alone had seen, or else the memory of it was holding him frightened and silent. Cherry explained to Charlie that Gene's vocal chords were all right but that people can be stricken temporarily blind, deaf, or mute by shock.

"It's almost a psychological mystery," she murmured.

Charlie vigorously shook his head. "It looks to me like a mechanical mystery. That strange kind of metal fragment—it must mean a new kind of smokeless shell. Maybe a new metal, or a new chemical. Or both? And the way you said it acted—little holes entering, a big hole at the back." Charlie puzzled over various answers. But Cherry could see her brother was not satisfied.

"Besides," Charlie went on, "where did the shell come from? Planes? But we saw no planes and, believe me, we were watching. Hidden on land? Hidden on camouflaged ships? Funny. There didn't seem to be any flak."

But even between them, Cherry and Charlie had only incomplete, contradictory, cloudy impressions of what had befallen Gene.

Suddenly Charlie pounded his fist on the desk. "What am I thinking of? Talking of mechanical—and

I forget to tell you the most important thing of all! Gene is a gun expert. He's one of the most valuable men in the flight forces. He's irreplaceable! And he's going to be needed for—he must be cured in time for—Oh, gosh, I shouldn't be telling this! Not even to my own sister!"

Cherry said evenly, "Tell me as little as you can."

Charlie grinned. "Thanks. You're a real pal. Well, you hear the guns, and you see us bringing in ammunition. You've guessed for yourself that something big is coming. The date is set. Gene is slated to play a key role. The Transport Command is lending him to the combat air forces. He has a special mission. We might lose without him. Cherry, you *have* to get him cured—if you can cure him at all—within a month."

"Yes, sir," Cherry said. "Within a month, sir. I take that as an order." Her tone was light but her determination was deadly serious.

Then they went out into the hot, starry night, through the chigger-infested palms. It did not seem like the third week in March. They headed for the silent soldier's tent. As they walked over, Charlie told Cherry:

"Maybe Gene *is* suffering from shock at whatever he alone saw or experienced. But I want you to know this. His silence is not the result of fear. He is the bravest, steadiest man in our crew. They don't come any better than Gene. And if *he* can be shocked into silence, then this strange new thing must be something really dangerous."

"All the more reason," said Cherry, trying to keep her own courage steady, "why we must keep and use our heads!" She was glad her brother was here to help her. "Maybe," she said, lifting the canvas flap into the private room, "maybe when Gene sees you, Charlie, he will talk."

The little, crude room was quiet and almost dark, lighted by a lantern. The corpsman at the bedside rose as Cherry and her brother came in. The silent airman saw them from the high bed; he moved his head a little on the pillow. Cherry told the corpsman he might go off duty now, and he left. She and Charlie went over to the bed.

"Hello, Gene," Charlie said in a cheerful voice. "How's the shoulder? Tough you had to get it."

The airman did not answer. His eyes clearly recognized his crew mate Charlie, but his expression did not change. Charlie struggled to pretend nothing was wrong, and kept up a one-sided conversation. "We sure do miss you, Gene. Hurry up and get well, will you? We need you. I guess you remember a certain date."

The airman's lips moved, but no sound came. And then Cherry realized that his eyes were not on Charlie at all, but on herself, standing behind her brother. He looked at her like a dependent child.

She forced a smile. "Charlie told me you're a pilot and an expert gunner. And he—" Cherry hesitated, then decided to risk mentioning the dread subject "—he told me all he could about what happened when you were hit."

The flier's eyes flickered nervously, but remained focused on Cherry's face. She tried to continue, to make this sound like a normal conversation, but it was eerie talking to someone who never answered. Charlie was so shaken he had turned his back to the bed.

"I think I'd better go, Cherry," her brother whispered "Maybe another time——"

She nodded and stepped outside the tent with Charlie. Clasping his hand tightly, she encouraged him, "Don't feel too bad about Gene, Charlie. We *will* find some way to help him!" Her brother silently returned her warm handclasp, turned quickly and disappeared into the dark.

It was very late by now, very quiet in the isolation tent. The flier was still lying there with his dark blue eyes wide open. His expression altered ever so slightly as Cherry softly re-entered. He looked as if he had been in some world of dream or memory, and returned to the present as Cherry approached his bed.

She smiled at him as cheerfully as she could, and said, "Aren't you getting sleepy by now? I think I'm going to give you a glass of milk."

She went over to the bedside table to get the thermos —her own precious thermos bottle—and poured a glass of cool milk, then a glass of water from the pitcher, to follow the milk. As her hands worked, her mind was at work too. She did not know much about psychoneurological nursing—except that the ancient Greek word, taken to pieces, meant the nursing of soul, nerves, and reason, and that it would require all her sympathy and imagination. After she had given the airman his milk and settled him more comfortably on the pillows, Cherry started to talk, with great care in her choice of words and ideas.

"Gene, Charlie and I know that something extraordinary happened to you. Now, look. We can't cure you until we figure out what happened, and clear it out of your memory. And I have an idea—" she looked into his eyes and knew he was relaxed and listening closely, "—that you are trying to remember. In fact, I think you can't quite remember, and that worries you, and so you are trying to reconstruct everything that happened. Isn't that right?"

She waited tensely. The soldier briefly closed his eyes to say Yes! Cherry caught her breath. Then she felt her way with her next sentence.

"And I think too that, while you are making an effort to remember, you are also trying to avoid the memory, because it is so horrible. You want to remember and get it straight, but still you would rather not think about it.

Isn't that right? So your mind is sort of—locked—between the two efforts. And that's why you can't talk. Isn't that right, Gene? Oh, Gene, try to tell me!"

The soldier uneasily turned his head on the pillow. He was breathing hard. What she had said had distressed him. "He wouldn't be so upset if I hadn't stumbled on the truth," Cherry thought. Suddenly she had an inspiration. She had never thought of it before, never tried it before, because until now, Gene had lacked the strength for even this.

"Gene, try this! Please, Gene, help me to help you!"

She pulled out of her voluminous pocket a pencil and a small pad of paper. Gently, she fitted the pencil into the boy's right hand, his good hand, and held the pad under it. She hoped he was strong enough to write. Yes, his fingers gripped the pencil and held it!

"Tell me what happened. Whatever bits you can remember. Write it. Write for Charlie, for me."

He looked deeply into her face, as if wondering whether he could trust her. Then his dark blue eyes dropped to the paper and slowly, painfully, the pencil started to move. Cherry's hand trembled as she held the pad for him. The pencil wrote, waited, wrote again, and slid off onto the blanket. The airman's face and hands were covered with perspiration but he had a look of infinite relief. He had written, in big, weak, clumsy letters:

"Concealed guns—maybe—I am trying——"

~~~~~~

CHAPTER VIII

Monkey and Other Business

THE TROUBLE WITH THIS PARTICULAR MONKEY BUSINESS was that it involved a real live monkey.

The girls were in their back yard, teasing Cherry and asking her what she was going to do about this new situation. Gwen, pinning pink panties neatly on a guy-line attached between the Ritz Stables and a palm tree, remarked:

"That monkey is a whole lot cuter and nicer than some people I know!"

Cherry lifted her dripping, soapy head from a bucket, where Vivian was giving her a shampoo. "I never said anything against the monkey. It's a lovely monkey. One of the best. Who am I to go around slandering a poor, innocent, helpless little monkey? It's just that——"

"Put your head down," Vivian commanded. "This is the Ritz Beauty Parlor. Monkeys not allowed here."

"I saw a doe and two doelets stroll into camp the other day," Josie Franklin offered conversationally, standing around in the hot sun.

"Not doelets, dear, fawns," Cherry sputtered, as Vivian firmly seized her by the hair and poured clear water mostly down the back of her neck.

"But about that monkey," Gwen relentlessly insisted.

"All right!" Cherry exclaimed. She got up from her knees, tied a towel turban-fashion about her head, and announced, "We will now settle that monkey business for once and for all!"

"We'll come along!" the girls chorused and trooped down the dusty, sandy road with her. "To make sure justice is done," Gwen said between her teeth.

"Monkey justice, I suppose," Cherry said disgustedly. "To be really fair, he deserves a jury of his peers."

"What's peers?" Josie Franklin asked, looking quizzical behind her glasses.

"Equals. In this case, a jury of monkeys. And a monkey judge," Cherry explained to naïve Josie. "If anyone says 'monkey' to me just once more——"

"Monk—" Gwen started.

Cherry chased her, in and out among the coconut trees. She could not catch her but Gwen did sober up.

The monkey in question belonged to Private First Class Joe Troy. He had caught the little creature, tamed it, and found a leather collar and a chain for it. Where he had gotten these was one of the minor mysteries of Pacific Island 14. It was amazing what articles the soldiers could rustle up, such as extra watch hands, springs for a bed, and a bass horn. The monkey, whom Private Troy had named Tojo to show his questionable estimation of the Japanese Emperor, always rode on his master's shoulder. The soldier had a lonely and difficult job: he was a G.I. spotter, sent out alone into the jungle to watch the sky for Jap planes. So Tojo's company meant a great deal to him. Cherry certainly did not want to take his pet away from him, but it had been impossible to find the source of infection that had sent Private Troy to the malaria ward. Monkeys can catch malaria too, and Cherry felt there was a vague chance that the soldier might have contracted malaria from his pet. The animal had been examined twice before, but no proof that Monkey Tojo was guilty had been found. There was no other source, in this case, to prove him guiltless, either. Meanwhile, other soldiers were taking care of the heartbroken monkey. No more boys had reported to the hospital—so far—with the headaches and feverishness and hot burning that spell malaria. But, to take no chances, Tojo had better go. It would be a move that would hardly add to Cherry's popularity, but an epidemic would not help matters either. Cherry felt badly about this. It would have been easier for her if she had been positive the monkey was a health menace, but she did not want to take the chance to wait for definite proof.

First, Cherry and her delegation went to see Private Troy and tell him that his pet's days were about to come to an end. Private Troy was too sick to care.

Then the stern, turbanned Chief Nurse and her party marched down to the barracks where Tojo was quartered. A howl went up from the men when Cherry took the monkey's temperature and pronounced him a suspect, as a carrier of disease. If the animal were ill with malaria, he probably could not be cured. The monkey did not like this examination: he blinked his tiny bright eyes and chattered angrily and tried to pull off Cherry's turban.

"Sorry, gentlemen," Cherry said, including the monkey too, "but Tojo is about to go to monkey heaven."

The boys called her unfeeling, hard-hearted, a murderess.

"You'll be dead if he isn't," Cherry warned them. "Malaria is nothing to monkey with—and that's not a pun. I mean it."

She was sorry: the men here were so lonely and homesick that even a little animal could engage their affections.

One boy went up to the little brown animal and took its paw. "Prepare to meet your Maker," he said, making a horrid face at Cherry.

"Oh, come now!" Cherry said in exasperation, "You can find yourselves another monkey, one you're *sure* is healthy. Why don't you," she suggested with tongue in cheek, "hold burial services for this one?"

As a matter of fact, they did. The Chief Nurse did not attend. "I really feel like a meanie, this time," she confided to Gwen. "But it had to be done."

A number of other ticklish duties had to be done, and they fell on Cherry's shoulders. One of them was disciplining her nurses. The girls were not having an easy-time of it, and Cherry's carefulness that they always let her know just where they could be found, and that not more than ten per cent of them ever could leave the hospital area at one time, did not sweeten tempers. Then on top of that, she insisted on drilling them, in the heat, after a full day's work when their feet already were protesting.

"I don't like this any better than you do!" Cherry shouted as she stood before the line of girls in khaki coveralls and heavy shoes and helmets and gas masks. "I'd rather be sipping a soda or going to a movie, too! But if the Jap planes come over, we've got to be ready and in practice to take care of ourselves."

So they wearily drilled, and Cherry drilled most of all. For she took the girls in relays of twenty, so with sixty nurses, she herself drilled three times, to each regular nurse's one time. Cherry did not feel exactly gay.

When her half-day off a week, and her full day off a month, rolled around, the Chief Nurse was always too busy to take time off. She worked right through her so-called free time.

As a grand and gloomy climax, it rained. It was the end of March, the beginning of April, and supposedly the rainy season was about over. But the rain came down in torrents, flattening the convalescents' vegetable gardens and the wild orchids Ann had just planted around the Ritz Stables and her own ward. Tents tugged at their moorings in the lashing rain, and one did blow away, with Cherry and her girls chasing it like drenched demons. The high surf broke loose two barges and they washed up on their beach. Little, friendly lizards climbed up their screens and had to be discouraged from such neighborliness. The ward tents got wet and would not dry out, and Cherry worried about her patients. There was no use worrying about wet floors, nor about the mud that everyone carried in large cakes on his shoes. It rained till the roads were all ditches, the sopping palms drooped like weeping women, and nobody cared whether tomorrow ever came—for tomorrow it probably would be raining again.

Cherry had once thought these tropical storms were picturesque, but after she had struggled, with the help of the corpsmen, to clean up the half-drowned tent wards, she thought of rain in a class with measles, toothaches, and those pesky, ever-biting chiggers. When the watery fury finally slowed down and dripped to a stop, the dampness brought out insects in armies. Cherry and the corpsmen and extra volunteers worked long hours spraying the swampy greenery with anti-malaria spray.

Then suddenly the sun came out. Everything still stayed wet, but after a day or two of blue skies and crimson flowering vines and bright-hued birds singing, everyone perked up again.

Except the Chief Nurse. For now, on top of Cherry's other ticklish jobs, Major Pierce made a new health rule for Island 14 and ordered Cherry to announce and enforce it. The rule was that, despite the intense heat, the patients had to wear long-sleeved, high-necked pajamas, and well soldiers had to wear *all* their clothing—not only outer shirts but every article they possessed, right down to leggings and gloves and buttoned collars—to foil this onslaught of disease-laden insects. Cherry, tacking signs to this effect on trees, and dodging the bitter complaints of sweating boys, remarked to herself:

"An executive's job is no bargain. Who loves an executive? Nobody!" She pulled down her helmet, pulled on her own gloves, and groaned to her nurses, "When we say we're sweating out this war in the jungle, boy, you can take that literally!"

"If you think we can grouse and gripe," Gwen advised her, "you should hear the G.I.'s!"

But Cherry's chief worry was about Charlie. She was concerned about his inability—and his crew's—to answer the Intelligence Officer's interrogations. Charlie was away now. Cherry suspected that he was spending at least part of his time on Island 13, with Captain May, though she heard the deep roar of transport planes at night. Cherry knew how troubled Charlie was about these fruitless questionings, and especially about Gene's condition and learning what had happened. Cherry wished she could help her brother. If only she could solve this mystery—even find just one clue!

The mystery seemed to be at a standstill. Nothing developed, that Cherry could learn of, from Colonel Pillsbee's possession of the shrapnel fragments. Most disappointing of all, Gene had had a relapse. It was a purely physical relapse—he had caught cold somehow. He was more cheerful now but too weak to be questioned. Cherry had to be content to let the airman rest and gain physical strength, before she could hope for him to talk, or even write again. She had been playing the victrola, borrowed from the recreation room, and the music seemed to help him. Once he had even smiled. And his shoulder was coming along very well. But all this brought the mystery no closer to its solution. Cherry could only wait.

One custom on this island, at twilight just before the bugles blew "chow," was faithfully followed. Soldiers and corpsmen and sometimes a few adventurous nurses climbed to the top branches of the tallest trees and looked out over the sunset sea to see if perhaps the mail speedboat was coming over from Janeway. The men had had no mail for two months, except for the little V-mail Charlie had been able to fly in. But not all the men's families used V-mail. Still, they never failed to climb the trees hopefully. Cherry felt sorry to see this pathetic, wasted ceremony, evening after evening. But this particular twilight, one corpsman, atop the tallest palm, shouted:

"The mail boat! I see the motorboat! Mail! Mail, everybody!"

It seemed to Cherry that the whole island came running. Bugles blew for Mess but no one went near the mess halls. Everyone on the island, including the officers, ran down on the beach, pressing forward as the speedboat cut through the water and shoved up in the slack tide. Eager boys waded out and pulled the small boat in, and huge duffel bags of mail were hastily passed from arm to arm, to be dumped on the sand.

Cherry was as eager as anyone else to get her mail, but the scenes going on around her snared her attention. The soldiers were so happy that the mail had arrived, so eager and clamorous as they pushed forward to help sort it and hear names called, so pathetically afraid there might be no mail for them after all. When the boys heard their names, they ran forward shouting, "That's for me! Here I am! Oh, boy, let me have it!" They dashed for the precious letters and packages, then suddenly came to a stone-still halt, not even bothering to move away, as they immediately tore open the letters and bent their heads to read. All over the beach several hundred boys stood, each one alone, hungrily reading those letters, smiling or frowning as they read, wistfully studying enclosed snapshots. Boys who had received packages immediately were surrounded by ten or twelve other boys, who politely offered to carry the bundles and made it clear they were going to stick around when the cake or candy or soap or razor blades or magazines or cigarettes were unwrapped. The owners of the packages grinned good-naturedly; the packages were understood to be more or less community property. Here and there, a soldier who had received no mail, went up to the mail clerks, whispered an anxious question, and turned away forlornly, empty-handed. Cherry saw several of those boys turn away with tears in their eyes: big, husky youngsters who had seen battle and who were not afraid of anything, except being forgotten at home. There were some funny things, too. Someone had received not candy but vitamins, and Miltie was opening still another fruitcake from his wife. Cherry stood with her own letters in her hand, thoughtfully watching this strange, touching, reading crowd on the beach, as the sun rapidly sank into the cobalt water. She thought mail call was the happiest and saddest day in camp.

Cherry was about to open her own mail when she saw men bringing huge crates from a Higgins boat onto the beach. The letters on the crates caught her eye. Some of them held precious dried blood plasma. Civilians donated and sent their own blood to their wounded sons and brothers and husbands and sweethearts. Cherry thought what dramatic proof this was of the tie and love between Americans at home and Americans away fighting. But she did not like the words she saw stamped on one crate. It was labeled "Purple Hearts," the medal given to those wounded in action. It was a terrible reminder that many men, going into battle sound and strong and vigorous, would probably be carried out on stretchers. Cherry shuddered. "I hate war," she thought. "War is no exciting adventure—it's the most horrible thing in the world."

With a sigh, she turned at last to her own letters and sat down in the warm sand to read them. There were several letters from her mother, and Cherry brightened as she read them. Her mother wrote that Hilton was just the same, still under snow, and she was having the downstairs rooms re-papered. "The living room paper is blue, with a dainty silver sprig in it. Dad argued with me to have it papered in red—can you imagine! . . . Everyone asks after you. You are quite the town heroine. . . . I've had several letters from Charles but no hint as to where he is." Cherry smiled at that. Their mother would be receiving soon, perhaps was reading at this very instant, her letter saying that Charlie was right here with his sister! Home sounded reassuringly normal, but very far away, very remote now. The bugles blew "chow" again, with a warning final ring, and Cherry walked up the beach to Mess, still reading. "I am working as a nurse's aide in Hilton Clinic, and Midge volunteered to do occupational therapy in arts and crafts. She will write you herself." Her mother asked if there was anything Cherry wanted them to send, exhorted her to take care of herself, "and do wear your rubbers when it rains." That was amusing, in view of the violence of tropical rainstorms. "Much love from Dad and me, Mother."

Midge's letter, propped against Cherry's cup on the rough mess hall table, was livelier. Midge had written in her sprawling, teen-age hand:

"I have decided something terribly important. Don't swoon. I think Midge is not a very dignified name, since I am practically grown up now. So I'm going to ask every-one to call me Madge. Don't you think that's right, Cherry? Don't forget—Madge, not Midge. But it's still me, and if you forget, I won't be angry. I wish I'd been named LaVerne or Jacqueline or Daphne or something romantic. Why, oh why, do parents pick out sensible names like Margaret? Anyway, don't forget, it's Miss Madge Fortune."

Cherry chuckled understandingly and turned the pages of Midge's letter. The paper was pink, the ink violet. It occurred to Cherry that, if madcap Midge was paying attention to such fancy little feminine trifles as these, she really must be growing up. Suddenly Cherry lifted the paper to her nose. Sure enough! Midge— Madge—had perfumed it! Cherry laughed aloud, but it was approving laughter.

"What are you laughing at all by yourself?" Vivian inquired across the mess table. "Don't you know people who do that go for a ride in a little wagon with a bell on it?"

"Listen to this!" Cherry retorted, and read aloud to the girls from Midge's—Madge's—letter:

"Do you remember our friend Kitty Loomis? She lives in that big red brick house on Fine Street. Well, she just joined the U.S. Cadet Nurse Corps. I am green with envy because she is lucky enough to be seventeen, the youngest age you can be to get that free nurse's training. She's already packing to go off to a New York hospital, right after high school graduation at the end of January, and she's so important I can hardly stand it. But I guess Kitty has a right to be proud, because only the girls in the upper third of their high school class can enter the Cadet Nurse Corps. She took all the right high school courses for nursing, too. It certainly is an honor. Golly, if I ever escape from high school, I'm going to try for the Cadet Nurses. I'm bound and determined to have a profession and go places like you, Cherry!"

Pink paper and violet ink and perfume—from Midge to Madge—ambitions to make her way in the world— and a definite plan as to how to win a proud profession for herself—"My little friend is really growing up," Cherry thought, as she folded and put away Madge Fortune's letter.

Two letters Cherry saved to read later that evening, when she could be more or less alone in the Medical Headquarters tent. One was from Dr. Joseph Fortune, the other from Cherry's very good friend, Lex. Cherry lit the lantern on her desk, dropped the canvas door flap for privacy, shooed away the insects for the moment, and started to read the closely written pages.

Dr. Joe's was the small, precise handwriting of a scientist. It was typical of him that he started with mention of his medical research work.

"Not a great deal that I am permitted to write you. Lex and I are still here at Bethesda, studying tropical medicine." Bethesda, Cherry knew, is near Washington, D.C. and is the laboratory center of the U.S. Public Health Service. Dr. Joe was working to discover new medicines and treatments. Then Dr. Joe went on to write of his astonishment at the changes in his daughter.

His letter had none of the elderly doctor's own gentle humor and glowing idealism. Dr. Joe just did not manage to get himself into a letter. She turned to young Captain Lex Upham's letter, knowing that Lex, whether in person or on paper, was always what the girls had called him at Spencer—a cyclone.

"Why haven't you written to me oftener?" he started out explosively. "I don't care how busy you are—I'm busy too. I might as well admit that I miss you. And if you don't miss me too, then you certainly owe me an explanation!" Cherry grinned. That was Lex, all right—highhanded and aggressive, and underneath nice as pie. "Sent you some presents, with the permission of your postal branch, things I thought you'd need, not silly girl stuff. Tinned orange juice, toothbrushes and powder, combs, and I broke down and sent you a bracelet too." Cherry chuckled. Trust Lex to figure out the things she really needed—and to give in and send a bracelet, anyway! About the work he was doing with Dr. Joe, he wrote, "I know it's essential but between you and me, Cherry, I'd rather have a gun in my hands." But Cherry knew Lex was more valuable right where he was. His letter finished up, "No use my writing you a lot of love stuff. I never was any good at it, anyhow. Tell you that when I see you. Whenever that may be. I just hope you're safe and well, Cherry. Don't forget me for any of those soldiers you're taking care of."

"No, Lex, it isn't likely that I'll forget you," Cherry thought. "The soldiers here are fine boys, but you, Captain Lex, are unique!"

She strolled back dreamily to the Ritz Stables, thinking how nice it would be to see Lex right now, even for half an hour. She missed him. And she certainly could use his help with this mystery. Lex's warm understanding always had taken the form of helping Cherry, no matter what risks he had had to face.

As she entered Nurses' Quarters, she found lights were out and most of the girls were snugly tucked in their cots.

"Cherry!" It was Ann's voice.

Cherry groped her way in the dark to Ann's cot and sat down on its edge. The two girls talked in whispers.

"Did you get a letter from Lex?"

"Mm-hmm. A nice, affectionate letter, bawling me out and giving me orders."

Ann laughed softly. She alone of all the girls at Spencer Nursing School, except Cherry, had been unafraid of the brilliant Dr. Upham. She whispered, "I got a letter from Jack. He keeps writing about when we're going to be married. Oh, Cherry, I wonder if he'll ever——"

Cherry waited. "Wonder what, Annie?"

"Bend down." Cherry put her ear close to Ann's lips. "From Jack's new APO address on this letter and from something I heard this week, I know that—Jack's not very far away from this island. And so I know he may— take part in the big battle up forward that everybody knows is coming."

"Oh." Cherry found Ann's hand, with the small winking engagement diamond on it, and squeezed it. "Don't worry, Ann. Please don't. It doesn't do any good. At least you and Jack are in the same part of the world, even if you can't see each other. At least we nurses are close by where the fighting is, so we can *really* help."

"I wish," Ann whispered, "I could be right up there where we hear the guns."

"Me too. Maybe we will be, yet!" Cherry answered adventurously. "I just wish——"

She never finished her sentence, for a pillow came hurtling at her out of the dark and knocked the breath out of her.

"All right, I guess I can take a slight hint," Cherry said with mock indignation.

She too climbed into her cot but, before she settled down, she thoughtfully returned Gwen's pillow—in the same manner. There was a squeal, and several assorted giggles, then, presently, only the buzz of insects. Cherry lay there, half-dozing, relaxed by the soothing hum of the creatures outside. Suddenly the hum grew louder and louder. Planes! Cherry grew suddenly wide awake. The sound of the busy motors mingled with the rumble of distant guns started her wondering again about the mystery of Gene. These sounds of war, so very close, made her fully aware of the importance of solving the mystery quickly. She began to review in her mind the meager facts which she and Charlie had gleaned—step by step. First, the operation and the strange wound. Vividly in her mind's eye she assisted again at the operation, and saw the strange metal as it was carefully extracted from the wound—piece by piece.

"Heavens!" she exclaimed in alarm. "Those two fragments that poor Bessie had overlooked! What did I do with them?" She leaped off her cot and dashed to her footlocker. Frantically she dug into it and searched her coveralls, hoping and praying that they were still there. She breathed a sigh of relief when her fingers discovered the two precious bits of metal safely nestled in the corner of her pocket.

"What do I do now!" Cherry wondered. "If I report this, poor Bessie will be disciplined." Frightened and shaken, she threw herself on her cot and tried to think. "Oh, if only Charlie were here! Perhaps we could figure a way out!" Then, too exhausted to think any further, she fell into a restless, fitful sleep.

~~~~~~

CHAPTER IX

Danger Ahead!

CHARLIE WAS BACK ON ISLAND 14 AGAIN. IT WAS A VERY excited and flushed Cherry who did not even stop to say hello but blurted out to him the story of the two fragments. "What will we do?" she wailed.

Charlie whistled softly. "Now that's a poser, but quiet down, Sis, so we can talk this over calmly."

"I have it!" exclaimed Charlie, after a moment. "With the aid of those two fragments and a close examination of the plane, maybe we'll be able to deduce something. It's just a hunch, but one worth trying! Where are the fragments?"

"Right here with me!" Reaching into her pocket, she pulled out a handkerchief, in one corner of which she had securely knotted the tiny pieces of metal. "I haven't dared to let these out of my sight!" she exclaimed breathlessly.

That was why Charlie and Cherry were setting out on this, her free evening, to the jungle spot where the plane was hidden.

"It's a shame," Charlie grumbled, as they groped their way out of the hospital area in the black-out. "She was all repaired and patched up the same day she got hit. Now we'll have a devil of a time finding any telltale marks on her."

"Better late than never," Cherry said, feeling her way along beside Charlie in the dark.

They groped along for a few minutes in silence. "Wonder what we'll find on her?" Charlie mused. "The repairs will show, they ought to tell us at least which direction the shots came from. Boy, it sure is dark here."

The total black-out these steamy, early April nights made the island especially dark. Everyone was being very careful about observing all cautionary measures, all black-out regulations. Not even a match was to be struck out-of-doors at night. For the dull roar of forward guns was growing more and more frequent. Yesterday, men, tired and unshaven, in mud-spattered, jungle-spotted suits, filtered onto the island, refusing to say where they had been. Right now, Cherry distinctly saw the flowering fireworks of tracer bullets over the fighting forward islands. Cherry wondered if the Japs might not bomb Island 14 one of these nights. Everyone half expected it. She asked Charlie what he thought.

He hesitated, and she wished she could see her brother's face, instead of only a pale blur in the gloom. At last he said, "It may be only a question of time."

They reached the road leading to the airport. It was deserted along here, eerily still. Charlie had left a jeep parked in a clump of trees. They found it and climbed in. Charlie drove slowly, for it was so dark you could not see the steering wheel in front of you, and the jeep's pin-point black-out lights threw only the faintest splash of light on the sandy road.

When they reached the camouflaged airport, they did not linger. They clambered out of the jeep, left it high up on the beach, and started for the fringe of palm trees. Even though they walked quickly, Cherry saw that something special was going on here. Through the darkness came the sounds of planes and trucks and men's voices. A shielded light flat on the sand showed her a man completely covered in an asbestos suit, mask, and gloves, squatting as he wielded a torch, welding two strips of metal net together.

Cherry followed her brother into the protective trees. They had barely entered when a tall figure rose and stopped them.

"Temporary command post," Charlie hissed at her under his breath.

Cherry stared but she could not make out anything but a hole in the ground and a field telephone slung over a coconut tree. The tall figure turned out to be Captain Keller, pilot and commander of Charlie's crew. Charlie explained something to him in a whisper, and he said, "Oh!" and came forward.

"Hello, Lieutenant," he said. "It's nice to see you again. How is Gene, our copilot and gun expert? We're all very anxious about him—for many reasons."

"He's better and he will be perfectly all right," Cherry reassured him, "*and soon.*"

She heard the young captain's sigh of relief. "Good girl! All right, Lieutenant Ames. *And* Lieutenant Ames! Go ahead."

The three of them saluted quickly, and Cherry followed her brother deeper into this secret camouflage area. She peered about, enjoying the adventure. Having a flier brother who could show her these things was a stroke of luck! She made out small planes—fighter planes—tucked away between and under trees. These sharp-nosed planes had horrid fangs painted on them, "enough to scare the Japs or anybody," Cherry thought. Men were working on some of these planes but Charlie impatiently hurried her past them. They hurried past the concealed hangar, too. Deeper and deeper into the woods they went, until they were in a patch of heavy jungle growth.

It was dank and evil-smelling here; the jungle was so dense the sun never penetrated. Though a take-off strip was cleared, there were plenty of scratchy, poisonous, hanging vines and undergrowth to dodge. Cherry hoped all this had been sprayed with anti-insect spray. They cut through a jungle defile and emerged on a grassy plain, edged by steep bare ridges. An armed sentry was patrolling up there on the ridge and Charlie called up to him. Then Charlie took Cherry's arm. "Look there!"

Cherry turned, and there, standing in the shadows, was the huge transport plane. It was so well hidden that Cherry might not have seen it had not Charlie showed her where to look. It loomed up like a spreading giant in the dark.

They walked over and stood under its enormous wings. Charlie patted the plane's side. "Good old Jinx. She's taken good care of me."

"So her name is Jinx, is it?" Cherry laughed softly. "In view of the mystery, Jinx is the right name for her." Charlie was not paying any attention but continued to run his hand lovingly over the wing edge.

"You act as if the plane were almost a person," Cherry teased.

"Well, she almost is, to us who fly her. She's definitely a personality. She's got her own quirks and we know just how she bucks angrily in a high wind, and how she purrs with pleasure when you take her up, even with a big load, and how she's lazy and doesn't like to hit over a hundred and fifty, and has to be coaxed. No two machines are exactly alike, Cherry. Machines are sensitive and individual, and respond to you just like people. Well, now let's have a look at her."

"Wait!" And Cherry told Charlie how she had managed to get the silent soldier to communicate, and what he had written. "Concealed guns—maybe," she repeated.

"Whew!" Charlie whistled under his breath. "That *would* be a discovery! Could that be what the Intelligence Officer is so darned worried about? He seems to have some other bits of information on his mind, too, that he's trying to fit together into a whole. Cherry, come on, let's see what we can find!"

They circled the great cargo plane, each with a blue-shaded flashlight, trying to decide the likeliest spot to study. The huge fuselage, or body, seemed to have no marks at all. There were no marks on the wide cabin door, either. Charlie pointed out the middle section, where Gene had gone back alone to check cargo. They decided the best procedure was to climb up on the wing and examine the fuselage more closely. Both of the Ames twins boosted themselves, by way of the wheels and landing gear supports, and up they went, catwalking along the port wing. They had catwalked plenty of fences and pierheads together, but this was very different. Outside the middle window where Gene had been, they got down on hands and knees, then lay down flat to study the plane area inch by inch. They searched minutely, with both eyes and fingers.

Cherry was the first to find something. "Look here, Charlie," she called softly. "Look at this!"

Up where the wing joined the fuselage, about amidship where Gene had been, Cherry's sharp eyes had picked out a tiny fragment of metal still embedded there. It was no bigger than a dime, and it seemed to be the same silvery metal they had removed from the flier's shoulder. A little farther back she found several other smaller fragments.

Charlie came crawling over to look. "Say, that's a find!" He studied the spots where the fragments had been lodged in the plane. "Look, maybe I can figure out the angle from which the shell was fired."

He climbed down to the ground quickly, Cherry right after him, and ran around to the starboard side of the plane. There he closely examined a patch on the fuselage. "Yes, yes!" he shouted. "Here it is! The shell went in here and after it burst, fragments came out on the other side."

Cherry looked at him puzzled.

Charlie explained. "If we know the angle at which the shell hits, we can usually tell where it came from— from the land or from the air or from the sea." He took a scrap of paper from his pocket and rapidly drew a diagram of what they had just found.

Cherry said uncertainly, "But isn't this more important—the fact that there are *two* kinds of marks on this plane, just as there were *two* in Gene's shoulder? Little marks where something went in and a big one where it came out?"

"Sure it's important. Hey! what did you say?" Charlie hesitated a moment. "It's the other way round, Cherry. The shell made one tear *going in*, but it left only those little fragments on the opposite side."

"Do you suppose that Gene was hit from the back, then?" Cherry asked. "I can't believe it."

"He must have been," Charlie answered.

"I still can't believe it." Cherry shook her head in bewilderment. "The doctors wouldn't have been mistaken. They've seen too many wounds." Cherry took from her coverall pocket the tiny bits of metal she had found in the plane and the two pieces she had inadvertently kept.

Charlie examined them again closely. "I'd like Gene to see these, too," he said. He straightened up thoughtfully. "Do you know what I think? I'm sure there must be a new chemical in that shell that leaves almost no solid residue after it explodes. I can't make head nor tail of this, and I'm the boy who's supposed to know something about guns. One thing is certain, Cherry— *the enemy has a new weapon.*"

Charlie jammed his flashlight into his pocket. "Whatever the enemy's new weapon is," he said, "it's a weapon of diabolical cunning. Smokeless, leaving almost no traces—it's the devil's own weapon."

Charlie led Cherry out of the camouflage area, back to the beach and the jeep. Driving back to the hospital area, neither of them said much, for both the Ames twins were thinking hard, trying to arrange these broken bits of facts.

When they reached the hospital area, Charlie turned to Cherry and said, "Guess we should report our findings to Captain May, but somehow I'd like to see Gene first and ask him what he makes of all this, and also show him this sketch. Can I see your patient?"

"I'll let you know the minute he's well enough for you to come," Cherry promised. "He's much better." They said an absent-minded good night. Cherry despaired of ever figuring out anything that had to do with such complicated mechanical facts as these. "Well, that's Charlie's department," she consoled herself. "My job is to get Gene to talk, and to cure him in time for his special secret mission. The time is growing short."

Luck was with her. Within the next few days, the silent flier improved more than she had dared hope. He would soon be able to get up, Dr. Willard said, and had him sit up every day and dangle his legs over the side of the bed, to prepare him for actually walking around. His shoulder was almost healed. But he was still very thin and weak, and needed more rest. He still had not spoken.

Late one afternoon Cherry dropped into the flier's isolation room and sent Ann and the corpsman off duty for their suppers. Gene's supper tray had just come in. Since he was actually smiling a little at Cherry, and sitting up in bed under his own power to receive the supper tray, Cherry was emboldened.

"How would you like to get out of bed and eat your supper in the chair?" she asked. "Feel strong enough to try?"

The flier nodded. Delighted, she bundled him into the hospital bathrobe, found slippers, and eased him onto his feet. He was taller than she had imagined, and he stretched his legs as if it felt good to be up again.

"Don't get too frisky all at once," Cherry laughed. "You can walk a little, then you must sit down."

With his good arm around her shoulder, they walked once, slowly, around the little room. Cherry felt, as any good nurse feels when her patient can get up, that this little stroll was a triumphal procession.

"Enough for now!" she said, easing the smiling flier into the chair. "Dinner is served!"

Because one arm was still clumsily bandaged, Cherry had to help him a little. She cut up some of the food, and spread the crackers with preserve for him. The flier nodded his thanks, with a twinkle in his grave, dark blue eyes. He held out the plate of crackers to her. Cherry made an exception of the rules and accepted a cracker, and munched and chatted companionably while he ate his supper. Suddenly he was tired, and Cherry had to help her patient back into bed.

She was bending over the bedside table, holding the empty tray, when a man's distant voice said, "Cherry!" She looked up startled, peering through the door of the tent. Who had called her? She turned to the bed, and was about to say, "Did you hear someone call me?" when she saw that Gene's lips were moving. Once more, he said, "Cherry!"

Crash went the tray on the floor, tin dishes flying in every direction!

"Oh, Gene! You're talking again! Hurray for you!"

He was smiling too, holding fast to her hand.

"I'm very much flattered," Cherry cried joyfully, "that the very first thing you said was *my name!*" The soldier nodded and his smile deepened, almost affectionately.

After that, the flier's progress was marked. Cherry urged him to talk, but with care and tact. Since music had helped Gene earlier, she tried music once more, using the victrola from the recreation room. She discovered that certain songs, especially melodious rhythmical songs, put him in a relaxed and cheerful mood. Then, when he was in that mood, Cherry would talk to him and occasionally ask him funny or tantalizing questions. He began to answer Yes and No. It was a big step.

Under Cherry's patient encouragement, and with the approval of watchful but unobtrusive Major Pierce, Gene began to talk in earnest. Not very much, at first, and with an effort, but he was talking. One of the first things he said was, "You've been awfully good to me, Cherry." Cherry was so touched, so moved, that she made a rather flustered remark about how nurses do take some slight interest in their patients.

Now that Gene was nearly himself again, fighting down the last traces of the chilling memory, Cherry did not make the mistake of believing him entirely cured. She realized he still needed encouragement to regain his poise, and most of all, he needed companionship. So she asked other convalescing, ambulatory patients in the hospital to stop by and visit with the flier. She mentioned this, too, to the nurses and the friendly young corpsmen. Everyone was willing and eager to help the patient they all had puzzled about, everyone wanted to make him feel he "belonged" again. Within the next few days, Gene's room became the most sociable place in the camp. Bessie Flanders was particularly sympathetic with him. There was always—within certain limited hours—someone there reading to Gene or chatting with him. His spirits rose quickly.

Partly to strengthen his disused arm, partly to keep his mind occupied, Cherry wished she could find some occupational therapy for the flier. If they had been at a big base hospital, either at home or abroad, there would have been a room for this purpose, with all sorts of things, like looms for weaving, leather to be made into handbags, materials for painting posters, and simple machinery for making novelties and gadgets. "Machinery," Cherry thought, "he'd like tinkering with machinery—or how about tinkering with a gun?" After all, guns were his hobby. And repairing a rifle would not only exercise his mind and muscles, Cherry realized; it might start him thinking constructively about the mystery!

Cherry borrowed a Garand rifle from an infantry lieutenant and presented it to Gene to fix. He was delighted.

"I know the Garand so well," he told Cherry in his reticent voice, "that I can take it apart and put it together again, blindfolded."

"Maybe I'll find you a more complicated gun problem," Cherry hinted.

Of course Major Pierce, and Captain Willard, too, supervised Cherry's therapy for the flier. They approved her handling of Lieutenant Grant's case. Gene steadily improved and at last Cherry sent word to her brother to come over to see Gene as soon as he had free time. Until Charlie could come, Cherry tried talking with Gene herself about the mystery. Like most soldiers, Gene was eager to talk about what had happened to him—as well as he could remember.

"Gene," Cherry said casually when he paused at one point, "do you remember how you were hit? I mean in the front or the back of the shoulder?"

"Why, in the front, I suppose, of course." His thin face was troubled.

"Never mind," Cherry said soothingly. "We'll talk more about it tomorrow." But she was more certain than ever that there was a new angle to the mystery of this strange shell.

When Charlie finally did get over to Island 14, the two boys had a happy reunion. Charlie was enormously relieved to see his friend and crew mate almost his old self again.

"Remember a certain date?" he asked Gene eagerly.

Gene nodded quietly. "I'll be there."

Cherry put in, "If your shoulder is all healed."

Gene turned full around to look down at her with those thoughtful, dark blue eyes. "Shoulder or no shoulder, I'll be there." Then he smiled, a little wanly, but it was a game smile. Looking at Charlie, he said, "Ames, I want to discuss this mystery business. Let's all three of us sit down and talk it over."

Charlie turned to Cherry, "Have you told Gene all the facts to date?"

"No," replied Cherry. "Not yet."

Gene looked eager for the information and Charlie rapidly explained what they had discovered and showed Gene the diagram of the plane.

"Charlie," said Cherry when her brother finished explaining about the fragments, "Gene is sure that the front of his shoulder was hit first. I'm sure, too."

Charlie thought for a long minute. Then he exclaimed, "That's it! Why didn't I see it before! Look, a shell is a hollow metal case. Inside it are small shrapnel balls and a bursting charge of some sort of powder. The whole shell tears one hole in the fuselage as it enters. The shock of hitting the plane sets off the bursting powder, the shell explodes and scatters the balls. Both the balls and the shell fragments cause damage to anything in their way. So far this shell acts pretty much like any other. That accounts for the big hole where it entered the plane and the small ones on the opposite side."

Cherry was growing more and more excited. "I think I see what you're getting at, Charlie."

Charlie grinned. "Now we come to the point. Suppose both the shell case and the shrapnel balls are made of some new explosive alloy that leaves almost no residue after it explodes. See?"

Gene nodded, but Cherry had to shake her head. It was not quite clear yet.

Charlie went on. "It's this way, Sis. The fragments we found in the plane were the residue from the shell case that burst as it entered the plane. There are probably more of them if anyone looks carefully enough. But the tiny balls went on and penetrated Gene's shoulder *from the front*. They exploded only after entering the flesh deeply. That accounts for the fact that the big hole was at the *back* of his shoulder."

Gene nodded again and this time Cherry did too.

"And if the explosive metal is smokeless to boot, you can see how mystified everybody would be. Right?" Charlie finished triumphantly. "Now, Gene, it's your turn."

Cherry sat very still at the edge of the bed, trying not to bounce in her excitement. Charlie, too, was leaning forward nervously for what Gene might finally disclose.

The flier, seated very erect in the chair in his bathrobe, looked oddly old for so young a man. He seemed to be trying to arrange his thoughts, frowning a little.

"In the first place," he started, "there *was* a plane. You were up front and looking forward, not sideways as I was. The rest of the crew didn't see it. I was slow in warning you on the interphone, because I'd been hit— apparently from quite a distance—and I was too stunned for a minute or two to talk. And you all were a little slow in looking around. Maybe you thought I was dreaming, or I guess we weren't expecting a plane just at that spot. Anyway, by the time you looked, the plane was gone."

Charlie's shrewd blue eyes were wide with disbelief. "Are you certain, partner? Must have been an awfully fast plane. I never heard of anything as fast as that."

"That's the point," Gene explained. "None of us ever heard of it. I was so surprised I almost didn't believe my own eyes. Because that plane was incredibly fast. And it fired from incredibly far away. Just before I—took sick, I learned of a new plane that the Nazis have. Special assignment given to a small group of us. It's very, very fast and mounts a new kind of rocket gun. That new gun fires shells of an extraordinary explosive force. Those planes and shells hum over the water making a sound like a bee. So we call that new plane—or at least that new gun and shell—the 'bumblebee.'"

"But," Cherry objected, "that's a German gun. We're fighting Japs on this side of the world."

Gene nodded in his quiet way. "Agreed. But why couldn't one enemy have a new weapon just as well as the other enemy? I don't say it's the same weapon. But maybe the Japs have a new gun or plane on the 'bumblebee' principle, or on a similar principle, Or a plane so built that a gun fires from an unexpected and therefore doubly dangerous angle." He indicated Charlie's sketch of where the Jinx was hit.

"Well, it's an idea, anyway," Charlie said. "It gives us a parallel idea, an example of how to approach our own problem. Go on."

"In the second place," Gene continued, "I think we were shot at not only by the plane which disappeared so fast, but by other guns too."

"Where?" Cherry demanded. "Land-based? On concealed or camouflaged ships lying close to land?"

Charlie said thoughtfully, "We were watching every mile of land and sea below us, and we didn't see any guns. Not even any smoke. Of course, guns could easily be camouflaged. And as for smoke, I'm positive now that this new shell is smokeless."

Cherry noticed that Gene was perspiring from nervousness, and she did not want her patient worn out. He could not afford to suffer a relapse, especially with the date of his mission so close now. So she said, pocketing the diagram:

"I think that's enough for this afternoon. Gene must rest now."

As usual, the nurse's word in the sickroom was law. Charlie obediently got to his feet, "I'm going straight to the Intelligence Officer with Gene's new information plus what we figured out. I want Captain May to have every scrap of information, and pronto! So long, kids, I'm off for the airport," and Charlie left them.

Cherry tucked Gene in. She should have left him alone to fall asleep, but they both were excitedly thinking about the plane.

"If the Jap plane I saw was based on land reasonably near by, that means——" Gene started.

At the same moment Cherry said, "If shells also came from land, as you think, forty minutes from here, then there must be——"

They stared at each other, thinking the same thing. Cherry tried to laugh but it was uneasy laughter.

"Then that means," Gene concluded soberly, "that there are Japs on Islands 20 or 21, where we thought there were no Japs! Japs secreted there, lying in wait for us! Man alive, we *have* stumbled onto something!"

"That settles it!" Cherry exclaimed. She started out of the flier's room as fast as she could go.

"Where are you going?" he called after her.

Cherry halted. "To the Commanding Officer to report this!"

He warned her, "But there's nothing definite to report! From what I've heard of him, this Colonel will ask you for a million proofs—and you have no proof at all!"

"Never mind that," Cherry said firmly, looking impatiently toward the command post hill. "At least I'm going to return these fragments and tell him everything

I know! Even if we can't explain the shots, we *can* deduce that there are Japs hiding on 20 or 21! And that's of more immediate importance—that's urgent!"

"Well, good luck," Gene called dubiously, as Cherry bolted out of the tent.

She ran up the hill, and into the railed enclosure. At the tent opening, she paused, scared. Maybe she was simply inviting trouble! But this was something which involved the safety of her patients, of the whole island! This might mean a surprise enemy action! At the very least, even on an off-chance, it should be reported! It would be flagrant denial of her duty if she kept still now!

"Yes, Lieutenant Ames?" Colonel Pillsbee was at his desk. He glanced up and dryly regarded her.

Cherry stepped through the doorway rather defensively. When she looked closely at the Colonel she realized he was ill. He was in full uniform and on the job but her trained nurse's knowledge told her that he was running a high temperature. Even his funny, bright yellow hair looked limp. What was it? From his voice, she guessed something was wrong with his throat— could it be bronchial fever? She roused herself from these speculations to answer the Commanding Officer's question.

"I have a confession to make, sir," Cherry started bravely. She took from her pocket the particles of metal and placed them on his desk.

"What's the meaning of this, Lieutenant Ames?" the Colonel gruffly demanded.

Cherry explained rapidly. She waited for Colonel Pillsbee to scold, but, perhaps because he was too ill, he merely nodded and skeptically waited for her to go on. She wished he would ask her to sit down, but he seemed in a hurry and let her stand there awkwardly.

"Well, it's this, Colonel Pillsbee," Cherry said, fighting to sound sensible and calm. "In the course of treating the wounded flier, several new facts came to light, which I feel you should know." She told him about the visit that she and Charles had made to the plane, what they had discovered and what Gene had told them. "Now that is all we know *for a fact*," Cherry said carefully. She was afraid he would not listen farther. "But I should like to mention, sir, the conclusions these facts seem to point to."

"Don't you think," Colonel Pillsbee said wryly, "that you might leave the interpretation of the facts to the Commanding Officer? Or to Captain May? However, continue, Lieutenant Ames."

Pretty fair of him, after all! Cherry thought gratefully and hurried on.

"These are the conclusions, sir—just possibilities— but, well, perhaps you would like to consider them." And Cherry told the Commanding Officer about the chances of a new enemy weapon, and the likelihood that enemy troops were hidden for a surprise attack on a forward island. She finished and waited, uneasily studying Colonel Pillsbee's feverish face.

"Very interesting, Lieutenant Ames," he observed. "Yes, I agree, such things are *possible*. It is also *possible* that the sun may fall out of the sky. But it is not very likely. My dear young lady, years of experience have taught me that it is necessary to be cautious and slow before leaping to any wild ideas. We must prove ideas before we believe in them."

Cautious and slow! At a moment like this! She had to make him see—she had to convince him! Desperately, she tried another tack.

"What do you think, sir, of the possibility of the enemy hiding on Islands 20 or 21, for a surprise attack?"

Colonel Pillsbee gave her an impatient glance, but he deigned to answer. "There again, Lieutenant, we do not have sufficient evidence to weigh, to be certain that that is a tenable viewpoint."

"But, sir—" Cherry swallowed hard and mustered up courage to speak out of turn to the Commander. "Even if there's just *one* chance, isn't it safer to——"

Colonel Pillsbee ran his hand over his forehead and eyes in such a gesture of illness and weariness that Cherry forbore to insist any more. Besides, she knew her duty stopped with reporting the information. The Commanding Officer would do whatever he saw fit for the security of this island. But his next words astonished her.

"Lieutenant Ames, believe me, I am just as deeply concerned about the safety of Island 14 as you are. For your peace of mind, let me say, however, that I consider your report and your so-called conclusions relatively unimportant, in view of—" he hesitated, then said with slow emphasis, "in view of other military action being planned."

Cherry hesitated, thinking. The "other military action being planned" was something she had already guessed from what she had seen at the airport at night, from the quantity of the supplies coming in, and from the special mission planned for Gene. Of course she did not know what it was, but it might be an offensive action. Well, perhaps that did put her information in the shade. It was true she did not have full knowledge of the military situation, as Colonel Pillsbee did, and perhaps if she saw her "mystery" facts in relation to the full story, they might be unimportant. But even so—even so—there might be immediate danger and the C.O. apparently was not going to do anything at all about it!

"You may consider the matter closed, Lieutenant Ames. Your participation ends here. Good afternoon."

He was dismissing her! Terribly discouraged, Cherry saluted and left. Her feet, carrying her slowly down the hill, felt like lead. She reported a secret weapon— the chance of hidden enemies—and Colonel Pillsbee promised only to think it over, and act slowly and cautiously! Cherry had confidence in the wisdom of the Commanding Officer's decisions, but this time, Old Safe and Sane might be too slow—and too late!

Cherry walked miserably along the edge of camp. She suddenly realized that she should call up the airport and tell her brother of Gene's and her further deductions. Charlie was probably reporting what he knew to the Intelligence Officer right now. Perhaps the Intelligence Officer would consider this more urgent than the Commanding Officer did! And if he should, Captain May was in a position to urge Colonel Pillsbee to take some immediate steps. Cherry felt as if a load had been lifted from her, and she ran all the way back to her own Headquarters tent.

The tent was deserted except for some corpsmen, working in a far corner, as she lifted the field telephone and tried to reach the airport.

There was a short wait, then a man's voice came through.

"Lieutenant Charles Ames, please," Cherry requested. "It's—it's rather urgent."

Again a wait. Then the man's voice said, "Lieutenant Ames is—well, he's not around." And Cherry heard the roar of a plane motor behind his voice.

"So Charlie is being sent on a flight, he's about to take off—and they can't tell me over the telephone.

But he wasn't scheduled for a flight!" Cherry thought to herself. She felt frightened and mixed-up. She said into the telephone, "Why is he being sent—I mean, is there still a few seconds to get an urgent message to him?"

The voice demanded sharply, "Who is this? And what is this urgent matter?"

Cherry said meekly that this was Lieutenant Ames's sister.

"Oh. Just a moment." There were voices conferring in the background, and then a different voice came over Cherry's field telephone.

"Hello, this is Captain May. Don't be alarmed about your brother. He is just taking the place of a man in another transport crew who fell ill. A routine flight. It's a sort of hurry-up, last-minute substitution."

"Thank you, Captain May," Cherry said gratefully. "Well, I guess that's all, then."

"You told the signalman you had an urgent message," Captain May caught her before she hung up. "Was it a personal message, or something you wish to relay?"

"It's not a personal message," Cherry said uneasily, "but it's nothing I dare relay over the telephone. It really is urgent." She hesitated, thinking what a golden chance this was to report the danger to the Intelligence Officer. But she remembered conscientiously that the

Commanding Officer had told her her part in the matter ended here.

But Captain May decided for her. His crisp voice said, "I'm going to be in the hospital area in about half an hour. Perhaps this is something I should hear about. I'll stop by to see you, Lieutenant Ames." And he hung up.

That was how Cherry, in spite of Colonel Pillsbee's instruction, came to tell the Intelligence Officer her own interpretation of the mystery. He pumped the information out of her. Cherry had no choice but to tell him. He already knew all the facts from Charlie, but facts only—it was Cherry who rashly leaped from those facts to conclusions. He listened acutely, his pencil jotting notes on the back of the diagram of the Jinx. She was half glad, half distressed, at the unorthodox thing she had done. It was dangerous to interfere in anything as vital as this, dangerous to incur the Colonel's wrath, but was it not more dangerous *not* to report this? What made up her mind was what Captain May said, after she had finished.

"I think your conclusions are right, Lieutenant Ames, proven or not. I'm going to Colonel Pillsbee at once. There may not be a minute to lose."

The matter was out of her hands now!

The next thing Cherry knew, she was called out of Mess and up the hill, for the bitterest rebuke she had ever had from Colonel Pillsbee.

"Not an hour after I give you orders, I find you have broken them!" Colonel Pillsbee fumed. He was as near to open anger as his rigid self-discipline and his ingrained politeness would permit.

Cherry shuddered. From his stern face, she knew this was the end.

"Unfortunately, Lieutenant Ames," he addressed her sternly, "this is not the first occasion on which I have found it necessary to reprimand you. But this time you have defied a major Army regulation." He paused, then slowly and deliberately announced:

"Your three-month probationary period is now up. You know that I, as well as Major Pierce, must write a report on you. Very well." His bony fingers tapped the desk. "I shall write to Washington, this very evening, to recommend that you be relieved of your post as Chief Nurse!"

But Colonel Pillsbee never wrote that letter. That evening, shortly after twilight, as soon as the first darkness came, guns roared and fire spat down from the sky. The enemy, whom Cherry had suspected to be in hiding, showed themselves with a vengeance. They opened an offensive attack on the Americans on the forward islands, and their deadly Zeros swooped down in the night and bombed Island 14.

~~~~~~

CHAPTER X

Under Fire

THROUGH THE NOISE AND SMOKE AND BLACKNESS, Cherry ran for the slit trench. She hurled herself flat in the dirt and grabbed the arm of the unseen person she had landed on.

"Any nurses in this trench?" Cherry gasped out.

"Yes!" Vivian shouted back. "Bertha and Marie and me."

"We've got to get to the patients!" Cherry jammed down her helmet, felt for the gas mask which the nurses carried at all times, and stood up in the shallow trench. A bursting shell screamed on the beach and Cherry's figure was silhouetted in its red light. "Come on!" she ordered.

She ran, with the three nurses stumbling behind her, through a wild confusion of flying dirt and smoke and whistling shells. She was not thinking; her previous military training automatically thought for her now. Her fear was a live, useful thing that drove her to animal caution against this crashing world. She had to marshal the nurses. Here was the terrible emergency for which they had drilled and organized. They had to get to the patients—to carry them out of the ward tents and into slit trenches. Were any of the tents hit?

Panting and choking, she peered over her shoulder to see Vivian and Marie and Bertha racing to their own wards. Their trousered figures in the broken light, bent half double, seemed to run in slow motion, so long did each terrible moment last under fire. Someone seized Cherry's arm. It was Captain Penrose, the corpsmen's commander.

"Ward 2 is hit! I've detailed twenty corpsmen over there, evacuating!" he yelled.

"Any killed?"

"No, don't think so." Another shell crashed on the beach and drowned out some of his words. "—corpsmen are all on the job—going to Ward 2 myself—you better go on to the other wards, Ames!"

"Right!" Cherry sprinted off toward the ward tents and huts huddled under the limp palm trees. The trees swayed and their fronds nearly brushed the ground under the roar of the wind which the buzzing, low-diving Jap planes had whirled up. Then there was a shattering roar from the beach, so loud and close that Cherry staggered. From the heart of the island came two more earth-shaking concussions that nearly deafened her. She suddenly realized, "That's our own anti-aircraft! That's our own heavy guns taking care of us!" Then she realized the unseen planes were fleeing and screaming away, out over the water. A great pillar of flame lifted from where Ward 2 had been.

Cherry's fear turned to fury. The beasts, inhuman killers! Bombing a hospital. Bombing the helpless wounded!

She ran, thinking faster than she ever had before, thinking clearly and purposefully. Never mind Ward 2. The corpsmen and Captain Penrose were taking care of that. She had to get to the other wards. Find out if any other ward was hit. How many casualties? Were any of the nurses wounded and unable to work? Was Operating Room left standing? How lucky that our anti-aircraft men had driven the strafing planes away before they had more than a minute or two to kill!

There was another terrific crash, screams, and Cherry inanely noticed that the white-gleaming radium hands on her wrist watch had stopped under the shattering explosion. As she entered the first ward, she heard the mighty roar of answering American anti-aircraft fire.

The ward was in good order. She hastened through the other wards and found that they were in good order, too. The nurses were tense and white-faced, but calm, and working fast to evacuate their patients. The soldier-patients, most of whom already had tasted enemy fire, lay stoically tight-lipped, as corpsmen lifted them from cots onto litters on the floor, ready to be taken out should it be necessary. From Ward 2, where the fire was almost extinguished, corpsmen were carrying out litters. A spare tent was rapidly going up near by to house these bombed-out patients. Anti-aircraft on Island 14 thundered, then lulled, repeatedly, and in the lulls it was possible to hear voices again. "Everything all right?" Cherry anxiously asked over and over again. And each brave nurse replied, "My ward is all right, Cherry!" Then Cherry saw to it that the nurses received supplies, and she started some of the corpsmen to taking records of the new admissions.

In this nightmare Cherry lost all track of time. It must have been an hour, or an hour and a half later, when Major Pierce called her. She went out of Mai Lee's tent and found him standing with one hand on his medical kit, the other on his pistol holster. He still wore a soiled operating coat, with kit and pistol strapped over it. He looked at Cherry with hard eyes.

"Captain Wilson—the young mess officer—he——"

Cherry did not want to ask. "He was hit?"

"He's dead."

Cherry's throat constricted. That nice, tall young Texan. He'd been so generous and friendly with everybody—he'd helped make their party a success. The Japs had killed him. Young Captain Wilson, with his friendly grin, dead.

Major Pierce kicked the broken earth with his foot. "There were three more killed. An anti-aircraft man down on the beach. An infantry messenger. And a corpsman. The corpsman—Max, you remember Max? —he ran out in the thick of it to save a patient. Nineteen years old, he was." Cherry saw then that tears ran down Major Pierce's face and he was not even aware of them. He said sharply:

"And this isn't the end. It is merely the beginning. Look there." He took her arm and led her down near the Operating hut, and pointed to the beach.

The night was quiet again, except for the clamor from the forward islands, and out of this scene of moonlight and hibiscus and lapping water came Higgins boats. They pushed up on the beach and dropped open their doors, to reveal litters of wounded men lying on the boat floor. Cherry and Major Pierce ran down on the sand. The men's spotted jungle suits were half torn off them, rough bandages bound heads and arms and legs. Their faces, in the half-dark, were dirty and sad and exhausted.

Nurses were needed to help here, but she dared not rob any of the wards. She flew into action. She opened her medical kit and uncapped her canteen. As fast as she could, she went from one prone man to another, examining him with quick eyes and hands. Every dazed, stricken face begged for help. But not one of the men complained or cried out. The wounded just lay silent and staring, only asking for water. One wounded boy with a bandage over his eyes said, "Gosh, an American nurse! I can tell by your voice—that sounds good." She tagged each man, to indicate what was wrong with him. To the most seriously hurt, she gave a shot of morphine to deaden the pain; threw blankets over those in shock; and directed the litter-bearers where to place the next wounded.

She smiled and encouraged as she worked, to cheer these suffering young men. They smiled back trustfully or even joked in faint voices. Some of them murmured that Cherry was the first American girl they had seen in a long, long time. Some of the boys were too shaken and shocked to talk. To them, Cherry murmured soothingly and gave sedatives. Some of them wanted to talk about what they had just seen and done, but Cherry would not let them waste their ebbing strength.

Doctors came running down to the barges just as another boat loaded with wounded scraped up on the sand. They, and Cherry too, gave the patients TAT, toxin and antitoxin to prevent infections, and MS, morphine sulphate, a sedative, and marked symbols on their foreheads with lipstick to show what had been given and what immediate treatment must be given. Corpsmen helped walking casualties to the wards. A truck cautiously backed down on the beach, amid the strewn men, and the litters were lifted in, to be driven to the wards.

Major Pierce plucked Cherry's sleeve. "Get extra beds ready," he said briefly. "Get blood plasma. Hot food. Shock tents. We'll be operating." He stayed there and helped to remove the wounded men from the boats, while Cherry ran to make preparations. She made two hasty stops on the way. She dropped in at Nurses' Quarters to strap on her musette bag, water canteen, and her web belt. Luckily she already had on her leggings over her slacks and heavy G.I. shoes.

Then she flew to Gene's tent. It was empty. Gene had gone! His shoulder was healed now and he had been kept on at the hospital solely to build up his weight and general resistance. But even so, he should not have gone before he was medically discharged!

No time to think about the flier! The new wounded on their litters were ranged in rows outside the ward tents, so many that Cherry wondered where to put them all. And Major Pierce had said this was only the beginning! Well, an evacuation hospital could take a thousand—and from the sound of forward guns, and still another barge of wounded pulling in, it looked as if they would have a thousand before this terrible night was over!

Corpsmen ran back and forth bringing blood plasma. Cherry saw haggard men revive as the life-giving blood was pumped into them. The stacks of empty yellow tin cans and paper containers grew larger and larger, and Cherry prayed that the plasma supply would hold out.

The casualties included almost every type of injury, with many head wounds from machine-gun and rifle bullets, shrapnel wounds, broken limbs, severe burns, and shock. Most of the wounded had had sulfa and morphine, given by heroic medical corpsmen under fire. And their speedy removal to the evacuation hospital would lessen their danger.

Within the next hour, Cherry put Ann and Gwen in charge of a hastily arranged shock tent, saw that the heavy influx of new wounded from battle were taken care of on the wards, sent Bessie and several other nurses over to Operating Room.

The nurses were working like demons—what with one nurse and three corpsmen to a ward of fifty or sixty patients. The nurses assisted the doctors and treated the soldiers. Cherry noticed gratefully that each nurse showed interest in each boy individually, asking or guessing where he was from, finding something comforting and encouraging to say. The first fright had gone and no one was paying any more attention to the forward firing than to thunder and lightning. They shared a warm feeling of comradeship in the face of danger. They joked and laughed as they worked and even some of the wounded joined in. One of the casualties said, "Want to hear what our orders were? It's this: 'Every Jap has been told that it is his duty to die for the Emperor. It is your duty to see that he does.' Pretty good order, huh? But there's a lot of Japs up forward we've got to plough through yet."

At Major Pierce's order, Cherry organized four surgical teams of doctors, nurses and corpsmen, a shock team, and a gas team, to go from ward to ward, to the men lying waiting outside the tents, and right down to the barges, to give immediate relief to the wounded. Cherry dared hope now that things were under control, for she noticed gratefully that the steady stream of newly wounded had stopped. But another part of her mind wondered frantically, "The Japs attacked the forward islands when they bombed us—how is the battle going? Are we winning or—or losing? Where's Charlie? Where's Gene?"

It was almost as if Major Pierce had heard her thoughts. He sent a corpsman for her, on the run, and she hurried down to the beach to join him.

"Look!" the unit director shouted, pointing to the black sky. Cherry did not see anything at first, then the sound told her. Jap strafing planes again! They were covering the thirty miles between the fighting island and the hospital island, and as their shells flared into unearthly light, Cherry saw they were aiming for the boatloads of wounded! They came closer to Island 14 now, and one boat dodged and veered out in the black water. The Jap planes roared closer and Cherry and Major Pierce and the others on the beach fled to the slit trenches.

Major Pierce, shaking his fist toward the sky, yelled, "The pigs! The pigs! I wouldn't believe it if I didn't see it! Strafing boats full of wounded!"

Cherry shouted back to the Major, "At least we got all the wounded off the beach!"

The earsplitting explosions of their own anti-aircraft left Cherry shaking. She peered around for fires but only one deserted supply shack was blazing. On the bare beach, shells rained down like a hailstorm. And then she saw a familiar figure, out there alone in the midst of the inferno.

It was Colonel Pillsbee, bareheaded, striding around with a map in his hand, directing the anti-aircraft fire, completely oblivious of the surrounding danger. Apparently he was directing other operations, too, for he was talking into the mouthpiece of a walkie-talkie strapped on his back.

After what seemed an eternity, the enemy planes were driven off and back went the hospital people to tow in the foundering Higgins boats. Miraculously, they had evaded the strafers. Cherry found she had lost track of time, as corpsmen ran up to unload the boats and she again made her pitiful sorting-out of the wounded. Someone told her it was half-past two. She could hardly believe that the night was so far gone. When she had tagged the last man and given him a drink of water, her thoughts turned to the nurses. She must get back to the wards and arrange to relieve her nurses! She could relieve at least a few at a time by staggering them. They had been on duty since three o'clock this afternoon—twelve hours—a few of them, who had extra emergency duty, since eight o'clock in the morning! The girls would drop with exhaustion!

Back on the wards, Cherry found everything going on as busily in the blacked-out, ripped-up camp as if it were normal, broad daylight. Wounded were still lying outside the Operating hut and the wards were overflowing with new patients. But every single one of Cherry's nurses, though pale and drawn, was calmly and cheerfully meeting the emergency!

Cherry darted into the various tents. The sight of Bertha working away, as unruffled as ever, steadied her. Cherry went on to have a look in at Operating hut. Extra tables were set up, so that rows of surgeons operated simultaneously.

"How's it going?" she whispered anxiously to Mrs. Flanders.

"All right." The older woman's hands moved rapidly getting out scissors, swabs, and cotton, for perhaps her twentieth operation that night. "We're using intravenous anaesthetic. Faster."

It was the same anaesthetic Cherry's Dr. Joe had invented! And they were using Dr. Joseph Fortune's discovery in jungle surgery!

Cherry figured out how to "stagger" nurses on duty, so they could all take turns at having meals and rest periods. But when she went onto the wards to tell the girls they could go off duty, the nurses refused to leave their patients.

"I'm not tired," Gwen insisted. "Honestly. Scram and let me work."

"Just wait till I help give six more transfusions," Mai Lee pleaded in her ward. "Then I'll go off for an hour— maybe."

"But how can I leave?" Vivian protested. "You know there aren't enough of us!"

"This is rough," Marie Swift admitted. "We've never worked with men brought straight from battle like this. They've always been cleaned up before we saw them. Go off duty? I should say not!"

Cherry gave up. She had hot food sent to them from the cook tent, which was working all night, and that was all the nurses would take time out for. Their humor and good health were carrying them through.

Cherry was exhausted, ready to drop. But she would not give in. She sensibly went to get herself some hot soup. In the cook tent she found Colonel Pillsbee and Major Pierce. The Colonel was flushed and soaking with feverish perspiration. Apparently the unit director was urging him to submit to medical care, for he was protesting, in his usual formal, measured way:

"It is an absurd suggestion. I simply have not the time to report myself in sick. By the way, Major, didn't I hear you ask for C type blood? Mine is C type, and I should be exceedingly glad——"

"Oh, no, sir, you can't!" Major Pierce exclaimed. "You're a sick man!"

"There's nothing wrong with me!" the Colonel replied gruffly and stalked out, a bit unsteadily, toward the Operating hut.

"He's amazing!" said Cherry.

Major Pierce shrugged. "What can you do with a man like that? Say, that soup is a good idea. Give me a cup too, Cook, will you? We're going to need this." With a cup of steaming soup in his hand, he said to Cherry, "Come on out here, Lieutenant Ames."

Cherry followed the surgeon outside in the dark. They found a toppled palm tree and sat down on it wearily.

"Now what, sir? I hope things are going a little better up front."

"Better! They're worse!" Major Pierce snorted. "Hasn't it struck you as strange that, although we can hear that the fighting is going right on, we aren't getting any more wounded here? We *know* there must be more wounded! Haven't you wondered, for the last hour, what's happening to those wounded over on that forward island? I'll tell you. We can't get them over here, and there they lie!"

"Oh, how horrible, Major! Can we *do* something?" Cherry cried.

Major Pierce plunged his hands deep into his pockets and took a long, deep breath. "Yes, Lieutenant, we can *and we will!* We'll go over to that forward island."

"Yes, sir!" said Cherry. "At once--please!" she pleaded.

"Right, Lieutenant, at once!" Then lowering his voice, he rapidly explained, "The fighting has shifted. Colonel Pillsbee just told me that the Japs are succeeding in establishing their beachheads. Our shore installations can't prevent them from landing. We haven't enough air support. So, with the Japs on and around the beaches, it's a physical impossibility to sail boats of wounded out of there. Now, I'll tell you what we're going to do." Major Pierce's anger had turned to steely resolve. "We're going to fly up forward to the wounded and get them out and fly them back to the hospital!"

"Have you arranged for a plane?" Cherry asked doubtfully.

"No—couldn't reach the Flight Surgeon on the field telephone—we'll just drive over to the airport and tell them they *have* to give us a plane and a pilot. We have Colonel Pillsbee's permission."

They left their empty cups in the cook tent and hurried to the Medical Headquarters tent. There was a gaping hole in its roof now, a burned smell, and a pit in the ground where a splinter of shell was buried.

Dr. Willard came in then, too. Major Pierce packed all sorts of medical instruments and concentrated medicines into a big black leather field kit. The three of them gathered up blood plasma containers and tubing, and blankets, and hurried to the Major's jeep.

"Maybe I'll see Gene," Cherry thought as they drove along in the fiery dark. "Oh, Lord, I hope Charlie is safe wherever he is! That could have been a short hop they sent him on—or a long hop—or he might be over Island 20 right this minute! Charlie, Charlie, wherever you are, good luck to you!"

This, her first taste of fire, was what Charlie had been through so many times. That thought made her proud, and steadied her.

Next thing she knew, the three of them were standing on the beach at the airport, while Major Pierce argued and pleaded for a plane. She looked around hoping she would get a glimpse of Charlie. Perhaps he might have returned. Impossible to find anyone on this dark, plane-crammed beach, in this milling but orderly crowd of men, with planes taking off so close that her black curls were blown back and her ears rang with the noise of the motors. The field and the sky overhead were thick with our planes. Out of dark distances— coming, Cherry realized, from the nearest airdromes— fighting planes of all descriptions were flying in to join the fight. Some of them must have flown very long distances.

A passing figure looked vaguely familiar to Cherry, and she seized the soldier's sleeve. It was a signalman she knew. She asked him if, by any chance, he knew where Lieutenant Charles Ames was. "I'm his sister," she explained. "I knew he was sent out but I have no idea where and I'm anxious for news of him!"

He smiled at Cherry and quickly set her mind at rest, "I don't know exactly where he's gone or where he is, but I do know he's not in this battle."

"Thanks for telling me. Is Gene, the pilot and gun expert, down here? The one from Captain Keller's crew who was wounded?"

"I wouldn't know, Lieutenant." The signalman was gone in the shadows.

Cherry took a backward glance at Major Pierce. He was still negotiating with the AAF men for plane and pilot. She had a few minutes to look for Gene. She suspected he must have come here. But where to find him? Ask at the hangar. She did that.

The grease-covered sergeant told her, "Yes, he's here. He's already been out once. Went out in a P–38 and came back in a sieve."

It took Cherry a few seconds to decipher this and understand that Gene had flown over the battle area, his plane had been shot up, but he had got back safely. He was here now! And he was probably going right out again!

Just then a tall figure in a leather flying jacket strode hurriedly by and the ground crewman grasped Cherry's arm. "There he goes, Lieutenant. On his way out again and in an awful hurry!" Cherry, dashing quickly after him, caught up with him.

"Gene!" she cried worriedly. "What do you mean by leaving the hospital without permission?"

Gene looked up gravely, and then grinned, as if Cherry should know better. He took her arm and guided her to the side of a dressing tent. They stood in the shadow of the tent, apart from the many men and planes and trucks surging by.

"You already went out to fight—" she started.

His look silenced her. "Of course I went out," he said quietly. "Do you think I'd stay behind when I'm needed? You knew you had to get me fixed up in time for a special mission. Well, Cherry, this isn't exactly the special mission I was slated for. We were planning to launch an attack. Instead, the Japs beat us to the draw." He put one hand on her shoulder. "Thanks for getting me ready in time."

Cherry looked into his dark blue eyes; they were black and burning tonight with intense purpose. His aquiline face was remarkably calm. Yes, she had helped him to get well, and in time. Remembering how much suffering he had endured only a short time ago, she marveled all the more at the tall quiet figure in the flying suit standing so determinedly by her side. He had gone through this inferno before, yet he was willing and eager to go right back into it. What courage! What spirit!

His hand, still on her shoulder, tightened. "Wish me good luck," he said. "I'll be coming back. You—you take care of yourself."

She watched him go with long, deliberate strides to the plane and climb in. In a flash of exploding light, she saw him wave, then pull down his goggles and duck his head. The propellers whirled, the motors sang, the plane rolled down the runway. Farther off, she saw it lift, gain speed and height, and streak away to the north.

Cherry stood there with her fists clenched in her coverall pockets, a grimy, sturdy little dirty-faced figure, with black curls curling around her metal helmet, watching the speck that was Gene. For the first time that terrible night, deeply moved by the courage of a man who had been wounded and deliberately returned to the fury of battle, Cherry wept.

Suddenly she remembered there was no time to cry and she hurried back to Major Pierce and Captain Willard.

"I couldn't get a plane," he told her flatly. "Well, I have another plan. Get in the jeep."

The three of them climbed in the jeep and drove back to the hospital area. As he drove, Major Pierce talked.

"It's the usual Jap sneak tricks. The painful truth is we're losing. Jap troop transport and landing barges managed to pass our Air and Naval patrols guarding those forward islands. They sneaked in in a surprise attack, using everything they had, and established air superiority. Our forces are trying to beat them off, back into the sea, but they are getting their beachheads firmly established. They're fighting on the beaches and from the battleships just offshore. Lord help our men! They're outnumbered. Reinforcements are coming but until they do come——"

Captain Willard said glumly from the back seat, "Only one good thing—in this inch by inch, single file, jungle fighting—at least we use hundreds and not thousands of men. But those wounded! There's no way of getting them out by boat. And planes are so precious they can't spare one for us."

"How terrible for those wounded men!" Cherry said very low.

"Well, we won't let it remain terrible," Major Pierce declared fiercely. Forcing a note of cheerfulness into his voice, he said with determination, "Don't let me for one minute hear anyone suggest we're licked. We're not licked. Our planes are coming in in greater numbers, and they're going to help us beat the Japs off those beaches and back into the sea yet!"

He cautiously pulled the jeep into the darkened hospital camp, braked it, and turned in his seat to the other two.

"If we can't get the wounded over here, we'll go over there and treat them. Since we can't get over by plane, we'll have to get there by boat. A small boat might conceivably sneak over to the fighting island under cover of darkness. I'm going out to organize a surgical team. Willard, you'll assist me. You come with me. Ames, you'll organize the wounded there. Be in Medical Headquarters tent with supplies for operating and an anaesthetist in ten minutes!"

"Yes, sir!" Cherry nearly sang it for joy. The dauntless Major Pierce was right—as long as they had courage and wits, the wounded *would* be taken care of!

As she quickly collected supplies, Cherry realized fully for the first time that she was going right up close to those bombarding Jap ships, right under those bombing Jap Nakajimas, within range of Jap soldiers themselves armed with rifles and bayonets—and that she very easily might never come out of it alive.

"I can't!" she thought wildly. "I can't! I'm afraid!" Then she caught herself sharply. She raged at herself, "You *have* to face these dangers. If we don't go over there and act as a field hospital, men will die. Whether you can or can't isn't even a question—you *must!* What did you have all that military training for, Ames, if not just exactly for this? You know how to take care of yourself under fire—you're trained for it! You're a soldier as well as a nurse, and don't you forget it! And don't you forget those wounded men! *They must be saved!*"

She came out of this session with her conscience feeling tough and sure. She ran and asked Bessie to come. Bessie agreed instantly. Cherry could have hugged her.

A Higgins boat was all that could be spared. The surgical team went aboard, loaded down with surgical supplies, a portable electric generator and machinery, blankets, plasma, medicines, anaesthetic, sterilizing chemicals. In the little band were Major Pierce, to be operating surgeon, Dr. Willard as his surgeon assistant, two enlisted men trained as medical technicians, Bessie Flanders as nurse-anaesthetist, and Cherry as organizer and operating nurse. Two corpsmen gave the boat a shove off the sand and they churned out into the night sea. Major Pierce steered.

They headed straight for the exploding lights ahead. But another danger worried them more. They would be on the water at least fifteen minutes, and already coral streaks appeared at the horizon line. If the sun rose before they could get their boat to the island and take cover, they would be outlined in the sun, an easy target for the enemy! It would be a race with the sun!

Major Pierce urged the boat ahead as fast as possible. No one talked, all anxiously watched the coral streak broaden and lift. The sea was heavy, the surf tossed their small craft from side to side. Above the engine beat and the lashing of water, the crashes ahead grew louder: they gained sight, now, of the embattled island. It looked unreal, encased in the thin blue shadows of before dawn. Then suddenly every tree, every leaf, every billow of smoke, was lighted up from underneath. The sun was climbing up over the curve of the world. It was so eerie, so primitive, Cherry thought the earth must have looked like this at the beginning of time.

But sunrise meant nothing so romantic to Major Pierce. It spelled danger, and he forced the boat ahead with every resource he had. Their Higgins boat scraped up on the sharp coral reef and lurched to a violent stop just as the sun burst in its full fiery glory. Major Pierce worked like mad to get the stalled boat off the reef before the Japs could spot them and fire on them. They lurched again, hit the water with a splash, and the boat cut through the tide to the beach. They climbed out into knee-deep water, seized their supplies, and dashed to the trees for cover.

"That little boat ride, my hearties," Major Pierce said with a grin, as they stood trembling in the wood, stopping to catch their breaths, "isn't exactly what I'd call a nice little excursion trip!"

Through breaks in the foliage, in several directions, the hospital people could see as well as hear snatches of the battle. In the lifting shadows and smoke and confusion, bursts of fire illumined running figures. Cherry saw a handful of men in muddy khaki clinging to a cavelike hillside hurling grenades—two soldiers darting wildly across the fiery path of a machine gun— more men in khaki and helmets crawling on their bellies, a great red cloud of smoke sweeping over them. It was incredibly slow, painful fighting for every contested step of ground. It was men fighting other men for their very lives. The snatches that Cherry saw left her stunned. So this was what our fighting men had to do! Jap ships and planes strafed the Americans holding this scrap of an island. The impact of the explosions bent the tall thin palm trees nearly double.

Cherry roused from watching when Major Pierce called out. Someone at a distance, with a blue flashlight, paled by the light of dawn, was signaling them to come forward. Apparently all this had been arranged for via field telephone. The hospital people struggled forward under the ragged palms.

A roar overhead, and the sky suddenly dense with planes bearing the white combat star, stopped them in their tracks and set them to cheering. Air support for the ground forces had come, in strength! The battle was decided now! But the fighting was by no means over, and more wounded would be brought to join the wounded already awaiting help.

They pushed forward again. Then two medical corpsmen of these fighting Infantry units came running. They guided the surgical team to a cleared area within a grove, a clearing station.

Wounded men were lying in crowded straggly rows on the earth. Some of them were bleeding profusely, few of them moved. A handful of medical corpsmen had set up a rough medical aid station and administered first aid. Flares of bursting shells lit up their haggard faces. Cherry took one quick look around and thought her heart would break. But the way these men could take it, the devotion of the corpsmen, and the surgical tent promptly going up, gave her courage.

She set about her own task of examining the wounded and marking lipstick symbols on their foreheads for the surgeons. Behind her, the two technicians gave preliminary drugs. The two surgeons were already washing up in powerful antiseptics, and Bessie was laying out the supplies and anaesthetic.

Now the team assembled in the tent. Stretcher-bearers brought in the first wounded man. They laid him on the rough operating table. Through the blowing canvas door flap the team could see the fire and smoke of battle. The thunder of big guns made the table tremble.

"Ready?" said Major Pierce. "Incision—clamp—ie——"

CHAPTER XI

~~~~~~

Happy Landings!

VICTORY HAD LEFT SUN AND A SOFTNESS IN THE AIR. Now, after four days of mopping up, Cherry and some of her nurses were relaxing on the beach. The ragged, bullet-pocked trees just behind them afforded more memories of recent battle than shade. But everyone was happy this golden morning, for now the American flag flew from the historic island, and from the captured Islands 20 and 21, which the Japs had held, as well. It was a great victory. To make them feel even better, fresh troops and supplies were coming over from Janeway today. Everybody was smiling—the soldiers and corpsmen who touched their caps to the nurses on the beach; clusters of patients sitting in wheel chairs or stretched out in the sunny sand; even the flowers seemed brighter and the Pacific bluer;

even a parrot which flew out of a tree had something happy to say.

"Let's play 'Going Home,'" Cherry suggested, rolling over on her other side. "When I go home I'm going to live on sodas and at the movies."

"When I go home," said Gwen, propping her red head on Cherry's knee, "I'm going to sleep till noon every morning. Ann? Ann!" She poked Ann.

Ann yawned. "Yes, my love. When I go home, I'm going to read. Read and read and read, everything I can lay my hands on."

"When I go home," Vivian echoed, "I'm going to wear silk dresses and high-heeled shoes and silly hats. And perfume. And jewelry. And—and veils."

Round the circle, the girls made their wishes. Cherry pushed herself up on one elbow, tossed back her dark curls, and regarded them with sparkling black eyes.

"Who wants to go home? There's a boat this afternoon. Speak up." "Not me!" they chorused in reply. "Uh-huh," she said. "You couldn't pry us out of the Nurse Corps with a billion dollars."

Cherry did not put it into words but, since that terrible night, the girls felt for each other—indeed, the whole camp felt—a closer and deeper affection than ever before. They had faced death together, nurses, doctors, corpsmen, soldiers, airmen, and now they were almost like one big family.

"Oh, there he is!" Ann was suddenly galvanized into life. The whole circle went helter-skelter as Ann picked herself up and ran to a young man waving to her from a short distance. The girls grinned sympathetically. They all had met Jack, Ann's fiancé, and they could not blame him for not wanting to be dragged over to "all those females."

"Cherry!" Ann called. "Could you come over here?"

Cherry joined them. She liked Jack, a tall, quiet, brown-haired young man. Curiously enough, he looked very much like Ann herself. Jack had come back from the fighting island.

"I know," Cherry said, anticipating their question. All the girls knew of Ann's long engagement to Jack. "There's a three-month waiting period for a nurse between the application to get married and the marriage itself." Both Ann and Jack blushed to their ears. Cherry grinned and continued relentlessly, "But the Chief Nurse can recommend to the Commanding Officer that such ban be waived. Well, what are we waiting for? What ho, to go see The Pill!"

On the way, it occurred to Cherry that it would be a good idea to get Major Pierce's permission as well. They found him in Medical Headquarters tent. He smiled broadly when they told him what they wanted.

"Sure," he said. "I'll even put it in writing. I have a grand wife and three youngsters of my own." Jack's blush was even deeper than before. Major Pierce grinned. "See my thinning hair, son? That's what lies ahead for a married man."

The three of them hurried off with Major Pierce's recommendation. But when they reached the command hill, their spirits sank and they walked into the railed tent sedately.

"No," Colonel Pillsbee said flatly to their request. "The rules must not be broken."

"But *please*—" Cherry begged, and gave him a dozen good reasons.

"No exceptions," the Colonel said flatly. "And I see no reason to argue the point further. Never mind, Lieutenant Ames," he stopped Cherry's renewed attempt. "Young people should know their place. Which reminds me that I have some unfinished business with you."

After this curt dismissal, Cherry marched out of the command tent and down the hill, too angry to talk. She tactfully left Ann and Jack to wander off alone. She felt really badly about them, and her temper raged in silence. The rules, the rules! Always the rules! Of all the exasperating people, The Pill was the worst! And yet, on the other hand, he could be utterly unselfish and self-forgetful, as he was the night of battle. Apparently he still intended to write that letter demoting her! Her troubles came back to her in a flood. "Well," Cherry thought, torn between resignation and fury, "if 1 haven't demonstrated my devotion and ability to him by *now*, there's nothing I can do to change his mind!"

Still not knowing what was to become of her, Cherry went on to the wards. She might be Chief Nurse only until Colonel Pillsbee wrote that letter, but in the meantime she had her job to do. This job was a happy one. With the aid of ward nurses, wounded men who were improving were being sent on to the base hospital on Janeway. It cheered Cherry to see them joyfully climb aboard trucks for the beach, waving triumphant goodbys, with their hands full of other boys' letters to mail. The last thing these soldiers said to the nurses was, "It sure did us good to know your hospital was near and standing by!" And several boys said, "There's nothing like a pat on the shoulder from an American nurse to help you get well. Thanks." Everyone in camp stopped work to watch the big launch, full of convalescing soldiers, putter off in the glittering blue water. That was a symbol of hope.

Cherry was at noon mess when someone hailed her from the door. It was Charlie. She excused herself and ran out to him. Her brother frowned and looked at her sharply.

"Are you all right?" he demanded.

"Just fine! What's the matter?"

"Are you *sure* you're all right, Sis?" It took several minutes to convince him. "Boy, when I heard in Australia what was going on up here—and I wasn't even here to keep an eye on you——!"

"Nurses are practically indestructible," Cherry assured him. She was bursting to tell him that Chief Nurses were destructible, however, by demotion. But she was not going to burden Charlie with her troubles. Anyway, Charlie was very happy with some news of his own.

"The whole camp will know it pretty soon, but wouldn't you like an advance bulletin?" her brother asked her, as they walked arm in arm along the coral-bordered road. "Flash! Ames News Service! It was just disclosed here by high authorities that with our taking Islands 20 and 21, the next move is still farther to the northwest and closer to the bombing of Tokyo. Flash! Flash! Infantry troops are at this moment packing up to leave Island 14 to move north for further action. They will be replaced by fresh troops to hold Island 14. Last-minute bulletin! The Army Air Forces combat group, in part, and the Air Transport Command group will also move northwest to establish another air base, and to——"

"You're going away!" Cherry cried. "Oh, Charlie, you're going!"

"Yes."

"So that's what you were leading up to."

"Well, honey, you knew one or the other of us had to go sooner or later. We were lucky to have as much time together as we did. Hey, are you sniffling?"

"Slight cold," Cherry fibbed. "Where—no, I won't ask that. Let's change the subject. Did you hear anything more about the mystery?"

"I will *show* you about the mystery," Charlie said gleefully. "In fact, Major Pierce sent me to get you."

He led her, of all places, into Colonel Pillsbee's command tent. The Colonel was there, stiffly pacing up and down, his yellow knob of hair bobbing. With him were Major Pierce, the Intelligence Officer, Gene, and the Infantry Captain. They were bending over, examining two guns: one looked like a large machine gun, the other resembled a small cannon.

"Harumph!" Colonel Pillsbee said when he saw Cherry. He introduced her to the Infantry Captain, then said, "We are about to hear a report on these captured enemy guns. Major Pierce insisted that the two Lieutenants Ames be present."

With icy politeness the Colonel offered everyone a folding chair. All but the Infantry Captain sat down. He stood beside the two guns and started to explain, addressing his remarks to Colonel Pillsbee and the Intelligence Officer. These three officers quite evidently had just been discussing and studying the guns.

"First I want to say," the Infantry Captain began, "that Lieutenant Cherry Ames's report to Captain May was of inestimable value." Cherry sat up, surprised, "The deduction of Lieutenant Ames and her patient pointed to the presence of Jap troops on Islands 20 and 21. That was correct. When the Japs sprang their surprise attack on us, it was not such a surprise after all. For thanks to the fact that Lieutenant Ames reported her suspicions to Captain May, and Captain May immediately reported it to Colonel Pillsbee, and the Colonel to me, I had my troops in instant readiness." Cherry's mind was in a whirl. "Therefore, Lieutenant Ames's report not only lessened the surprise, but also told us where the enemy was located and thus saved us invaluable time in meeting the attack! It is quite possible that we might not have won this engagement if Lieutenant Ames had not reported what she knew."

Colonel Pillsbee cleared his throat. "Not knew. Surmised."

The Infantry Captain said calmly, "Lieutenant Cherry Ames has rendered a great service—both Lieutenants Ames. They uncovered the existence of a deadly new enemy weapon. To continue, sir.

"Captain May had some partial information for which he was seeking the missing facts. When Lieutenant Ames made her report, she filled in those blanks. Therefore, in the recent battle, we knew we had to deal with this new enemy gun. We knew how best to combat it, for its surprise element was now lost. We knew, too, where to look for it on land and how to identify the new enemy plane which carries this gun.

"Now to examine the weapon itself." The Infantry Captain rested either hand on the two captured guns.

"A laboratory analysis of the fragments which were removed from the plane and from Lieutenant Grant's shoulder showed that a new chemical and a new metal alloy were used to create an extraordinary shell. As Lieutenant Charles Ames surmised, the shell is hollow and filled with shrapnel balls. The shell itself explodes and almost disappears on entering the plane. A further search of the plane revealed, as Lieutenant Charles Ames thought, that there were more fragments embedded in various places that had been overlooked. No one would have expected them to be so minute.

"The shrapnel balls inside the shell are very tiny. They are intended to travel on until they penetrate a solid body or strike some hard surface. Then they, too, explode almost without residue. This explains the flier's strange wounds—the tiny points made on entering and the big gash at the back. Fortunately he was far enough to one side to escape all except a few of the balls. The rest apparently struck a heavy piece of machinery in the cargo and spent themselves harmlessly."

The Captain paused and looked around as if to wait for any questions. Then he went on, "Further, such a shell is fired at tremendous speed, going faster and farther than an ordinary shell. Also it can be shot from a great distance, lessening the enemy's risk to himself. That fact, plus the extraordinary speed of the shell, and the specially fast plane shooting it, must be why Lieutenant Grant was confused in his impressions, and why the crew did not see the plane. Since the explosions are smokeless, no one could quite believe a shell had even been fired.

"I might explain," the captain added, "that the Japs make up this new chemical and alloy shell in *two* forms. One fits a gun somewhat larger than our machine guns. The other fits a small cannon. Both are of the same composition, but they do not resemble any other shells known to us in construction, size and character. They are lighter and of a new form. This is really a major discovery!

"Now, the new enemy cannon, here, is located on land. But a new type enemy plane carries the gun, here. This plane is very fast, has an unusually powerful engine, and has its gun placed at an unexpected and therefore unusually dangerous angle. We captured such a plane—that is, Lieutenant Ames," the Infantry Captain smiled at Cherry, "it was shot down by Lieutenant Grant here, whom you helped to recover."

Cherry's head was spinning in earnest now! Then the Infantry Captain, Major Pierce, Captain May and Lieutenant Grant were all shaking her and Charlie's hands, and the Intelligence Officer was saying, "You will receive a citation from Washington for your alertness, both of you!"

Colonel Pillsbee once more cleared his throat. "As to Lieutenant Cherry Ames," he said dryly. "I am aware that you were—er—useful."

Cherry held her breath as he continued.

"In view of the service which Lieutenant Cherry Ames has rendered, I herewith wish to say that I am sorry for my having doubted her seriousness of character and purpose. I feel that she has amply proven herself, if by nothing else than by her performance of duty as a nurse during the night of battle." The Colonel was apologizing handsomely. The Pill was sorry! The Pill was fair, and pretty nice at that!

"Therefore, Lieutenant Cherry Ames, you are no longer acting Chief Nurse, but Chief Nurse in full status and permanent post." He held out his hand. "Let me be the first to congratulate you on your winning this post and on your forthcoming citation."

Cherry shook his hand, and everyone else's hand, thinking wildly, "I'm vindicated! I'm cleared! I'm going to continue as Chief Nurse! And I—I'm going to receive an honor! All my idealism about nursing—I've actually managed to live up to it, I guess!"

She went out of that tent in a complete daze. The others, including Charlie, remained behind for further discussion, and she wandered around alone trying to digest these wonderful developments. As Cherry was walking down the road, someone called to her. It was Gene.

She hurried over to him and warmly congratulated him on shooting down the Jap plane.

He grinned, looking down at her. "Part your fault. You nursed me back to health, you know. Cherry, I want to say several things to you. Let's find a quiet place where we can talk."

Under a thicket of palm trees, away from the road, they sat down.

"I know one thing you're going to say," Cherry smiled regretfully. "Charlie told me you're all leaving."

Gene smiled back at her, "Yes. And I'm going along because all those things in my mind are straightened out now. Now that I know for sure, I'd like you to know too. The reason I was so shocked in the first place was this: in that split second when I saw a new enemy plane, and was hit in such a strange way, I realized the enemy must have a new weapon. Worse, I realized I—we— had nothing with which to fight it—not only that my transport was unarmed but that there was no American gun to meet this new enemy gun. I felt so—helpless. And then when I found no one else had seen this new thing, and didn't quite believe me, I was so terribly discouraged, and confused, and shaken, and well—you know."

Cherry nodded. "I understand, Gene," she said, warmly clasping his hand. "But now everything is all cleared up, isn't it, Gene?"

"Absolutely all cleared up!" the flier said joyously. He took her hand. "Thanks to you. Cherry, only a remarkable girl could have nursed me through that. I want to thank you with all my heart. You've been not only a good nurse, you've been a good friend to me as well. I'm certainly going to miss you," he added soberly.

Touched by Gene's sincerity, Cherry replied a little shakily, "Of course, we're good friends! We've gone through this difficult thing together, so naturally we feel great sympathy for each other. I'm sorry you're going away, Gene. But, Gene," Cherry's face brightened, "we'll all be seeing each other again, you and Charlie and I."

"Of course!" Gene regained his smile. "Of course we'll see each other again. Maybe we'll meet in a plane. There are such things as flying nurses, you know! But right now, I've got to say good-by. We're leaving immediately. In fact," he joked, "they've probably left without me!"

"So soon?" Cherry cried. They both got to their feet and hurried down the road. "Charlie, too? But I haven't said——"

"Say it now," Charlie called as he caught up with them and put his arms around Cherry. "So long, Sis. Wish me good luck."

Her brother kissed her lightly on the cheek. Cherry could not control the hot tears this time.

"Look," said Charlie steadily. His eyes were intensely blue in his sunburned, windburned face. "Ever see a snappy salute?" He saluted and snapped his fingers at the same time. They both managed a brief laugh. Then the two young men strode quickly toward the jeep that was waiting to take them to the airport. Cherry waved until they were out of sight.

She stumbled down the road and ran to the empty Operating hut to find Mrs. Flanders. "Oh, Bessie! Bessie!" she wailed and pillowed her head on the older woman's comforting shoulder. "Charlie's going and everything's happening and I'm all mixed up and excited!"

"Why, Cherry," Bessie said softly. "You've been a brave soldier all along. You've taken your troubles with Colonel Pillsbee in your stride, and you've done a grand job as Chief Nurse, and now you're all cleared and won a great honor and everything! So you really have a right to be proud! Besides, don't you hear the planes? Let's go out and see them!"

Cherry and Bessie ran to the beach. Other nurses and patients and hospital people came running too. Here came the planes, great roaring rows of them, in beautiful formation, flying into the sun! They soared and sang over Cherry's lifted head. And as she watched the magnificent planes fly proudly past, she vowed to herself:

"I'm going to be up there myself, flying and nursing, one of these days!"